ONLY ONE WAY OUT

A Mystery Novel

By Ruth Raby Moen

All the best!

Ruth Raby Moen

We ran a few yards down the ditch, just far enough to get clear. Casey hustled me along in front of him. He then stopped and gave me a quick peck on the cheek. "Don't look back. Just run," he said, and threw me, bodily, up the bank on the other side.

Less than a minute later, the tractor bashed into the pickup on the driver's side. The seat buckled, the crumbled door enmeshed into the dashboard.

I glanced back once, making sure Casey was still behind me, noting that the tractor could not climb the steep bank. I slowed, thinking I'd wait for him to catch up. But again, he shouted at me, gesturing wildly at the woods. "Go, dammit. Just go!"

This time, I did what I was told. I ran. Didn't look back, didn't ask questions, didn't stop to wonder why when Casey seemed to be lagging behind.

Just ran.

After about ten minutes, I could no longer hear his labored breathing behind me at all, only the tractor's screaming clash of gears and roaring groan of the engine.

Never mind. Can't think about that. Can't think about any of it right now.

Lungs heaving, side aching, I ran for all I was worth.

The fence and the old maple tree were dead ahead.

Other books by
Ruth Raby Moen

Hayseeds In My Hair; A Memoir
Deadly Deceptions, A Mystery Novel

All Flying Swan Publications are available at special discounts
for bulk purchases or to wholesalers/distributors. For details, write
to PO Box 46, Sedro-Woolley, WA 98284.

Published by;
Flying Swan Publications
PO Box 46
Sedro-Woolley, WA 98284

Dedicated to three sisters,
each one of which I love equally
and more than life itself.

Chapter

1

Rain, rain go away,
Little Kathy wants to play . . .

The drumming rain on the car's roof and the clack, swish, clack of the windshield wipers was making me crazy. *Damn this weather. As soon as I try to do something it rains.* And of course, it had to happen on Labor Day. My last three-day weekend this year.

My job as office manager at a prestigious Seattle law firm had me stressed to the max. I tend to be grouchy when I'm stressed and take it out on the closest and most convenient target.

Such as my boyfriend Casey.

He was convinced that a camping trip was just what I needed. A little R & R. And since I'd been wanting to head for the hills for some time, I had to agree. Yesterday morning, we decided it was now or never.

We were going north and east of Seattle, into the northern Cascade mountain range. These mountains, or so Casey claimed, were the closest thing to perfection this side of heaven. I was not convinced. So far, the only celestial forces I'd seen was this Gawd-awful rain.

Last week, Casey had accused me of being a 'city girl.' As if it were a crime to be civilized. Sophisticated. Of course, to him, any woman who doesn't need a bib to sip soup is sophisticated. But then, I suppose it's true. Up to this point, my wildest excursion had been a shop-till-you-drop trip to the local mall with a brand new $1,500-limit credit card.

We had left I-5 long ago and passed through the small town of Darrington, our last stop, just late enough for all the stores to be closed. "Damn," I muttered, drawing the collar up on my blue blazer and clicking the knob on the heater fan up a notch. "Where'd this storm come from? Didn't you check the weather report?"

"Not since yesterday," he replied, almost in a mumble and ducking his head as if he were dodging bullets. "I haven't had time."

At the tender age of fourteen, when the other girls in my class were obsessing over boys and dates and hairdos, my parents were getting a divorce. It taught me a lesson I never should have learned and ever since, I've had trouble with men. Trusting them, respecting them, and loving them. I usually loved them too much. Although each parent had blamed the other for their break-up, it became apparent, at least to me, that my father was a lost cause. Casey, in some ways, reminded me of him. Sometimes I was so head over heels in love I thought my heart would break. On other days, I could have chewed right through his jugular without a moment's hesitation.

This latest incident of neglect was one of those.

"Good grief, Casey. All you had to do was call the weather bureau. Of course you had time. You've had the whole day."

"What do you mean?" He steered around a rough spot in the road, jaw muscles working and breathing heavily through his nose. "I had to go all the way across town after some toilet paper, none of those stores around yer place know jack-shit about camping out. And then I had to get the car ready and get it packed. There's just not enough room in this heap. I told you we should have brought my old pick-up."

"Heap? My car's a heap? I'll have you know, Pond Scum, that a '75 Porsche is considered a classic. Not a heap. And I told you, I'm not riding in your old pick-up. It doesn't have a heater and it smells of pig poop."

10

"Aw, get off it Kate, I ain't raised no pigs since I was a kid. You know that."

Casey was noticeably offended. Too bad. I was drawing a deep breath, ready to expound on all the things to be found under my bathroom cabinet, including toilet paper, when a logging truck careened around a small turn. It barrelled down the mountain straight at us. Top heavy with fresh cut logs, it teetered for a moment on two wheels, brakes screaming, tires exploding like cannons.

I shrieked, and grabbed the dashboard.

The truck approached at a deadly speed. A black object hurled through the air and bounced with a thud off the grill of my car. As it snaked off to the side, I recognized it as a length of rubber peeled off the truck tire like an orange.

Casey jerked the steering wheel and veered out of its way.

We crested the shoulder of the road. The huge truck thundered by us with a blat and a rumble, its air horn shattering the still, wet air.

The Porsche was out of control. It jounced over a ditch, flinging rocks and dirt, and plowed into the soft earth on the other side. Even with my seat belt on, I was tossed around like a rag doll and bashed into the door. A sickening scrape of the car's underbelly on a large rock reacted on my nerves like a thumbnail screeched across a blackboard.

Just then, the road forked. "That's our turn," I said, pointing to the left. "Over there." Plowing through the brush, Casey maneuvered the car between two large stands of timber and around a mound of dirt meant to be a roadblock.

I saw no reason to be leaving the main artery and asked him about it. "Where're you going?" The car settled into an old road, not much more than two tire grooves with grass growing up the middle. "Casey, this is the wrong way. You're going to get us lost."

"It's all right," he said. "Just a detour. An old logging trail. It ought to meet us up with the state highway in just a little bit." I wasn't convinced but I hated having to argue with him. The car fishtailed up the muddy bank, crawling in second gear for several miles before sluicing through the water of a huge mud hole. Then it stalled.

We were stranded.

I peered out the side window, wincing from a painful bruise to my shoulder. "Holy shit, Casey. Look!" A large portion of the road had washed away, leaving a big hole where the right wheels would have gone. The car had come to a halt perilously close to the edge.

To my right a few feet and straight down, a river raged some hundred feet below. It crashed over the rocks and through the timbers, uprooting whole trees and snapping them like toothpicks. Farther down and behind me, the distant roar of a waterfall magnified the sound of the falling rain.

I shrunk into the seat and braced my feet against the glove compartment.

"I've had enough of this." Busy thumping the gas pedal and grinding the key in the ignition, he didn't answer. "Casey, let's go back."

The car's starter gnarled menacingly, then petered out to a wimpy groan. It was not going to start. The muscles in my neck tensed. As panic swelled up from my stomach, I thought I might have to vomit. "Did you hear me? I want to go home."

Casey switched off the key and pulled the brake. "Lines are wet," he said. "Stay here and don't be moving around a lot." Unfolding his long legs, he crawled out of the car and slammed the door.

Sitting on the edge of a cliff, waiting for Casey to get his act together, was not my idea of a vacation. "`Stay here', he says. You better believe I'll stay here. Let him get HIS scrawny butt soaked." I hated being dependant on someone else.

It made me feel vulnerable.

And even more grouchy.

For a long minute, I watched him fumble with the hood. The rain plastered his hair to his head in long, dark sheets. With a sideways jerk, he flopped it out of his face and stared at me through the window.

I shrugged my shoulders in a 'how do I know what you want' gesture. He rapped the hood with his knuckle and jabbed a finger towards the front panel. Quickly, I pulled the knob to release the hood latch, clucking at him for having forgotten.

It was getting dark. Overhead, a blob of grey sky was taking on the purple hue of the mountains, sopping it up like ink into a blotter. And with the dark silence came a terrible loneliness . . .

The hood was still up. I couldn't see him.

I cracked an opening in the window and stretched to reach it. "Casey. What are you doing?" He didn't answer. "Hey. What's wrong with my car?" Silence. Broken only by the battering sounds of wind and rain. "Can you fix it?"

No answer.

Good grief. Could he have fallen off the edge? Stepped too close and caused a small landslide?

It was possible. There was only about three feet of sandy soil between him and a wide, yawning canyon. I waited. Three minutes . . . five minutes . . . ten minutes . . . "Are you all right?"

Oh, God. Please, let him be OK. Please. I don't care about this car. Just let him . . . .

"Casey? Where are you?" In my mind's eye, I could see him shwooshing downriver in the rain, bashing into the rocks, fighting to keep his head up, to stay alive.

"Casey!"

Just then, the door on the driver's side yawed open, ushering in the wet and gusty storm. And my lover, my Sweet Darlin', my sometimes hero and soon-to-be fiance, flopped in the seat. "Brrr, it's cold." He rubbed his hands together and shivered. "What were you hollering about?"

I was never so glad to see someone in my life. But for some odd, bitchy reason, I didn't want him to know how frightened I'd been. "I . . . just wondered what was taking you so long. Look at you. You're sopping wet."

"Reach back there and get me a dry shirt."

Since it was too dark to see and I was already draped over the back of the car seat, I quietly found my box of tissue and blew my nose. Then, I looked for his shirt.

While I fumbled through boxes of cooking gear and sleeping bags, Casey continued trying to start the car. Again and again, he clicked the key in the ignition and stomped on the gas pedal. "Come on, car," he said. "Come on, baby. Start!"

Suddenly, with a quickening rumble and a banging cough out the back, it kicked in. Within minutes and with a mighty roar and a menacing knock, we had eased around the cleft in the road and headed up hill.

Leaning back on the head rest, I realized I'd been holding my breath. I exhaled noisily, and said, "Let's find a campsite. Anywhere. I've got to get out of this car."

It boomed and vroomed, then settled into a low growl as he wrestled the gear shift into second. "You know, this would be a nice car if you'd take care of it."

Staring out the window at the dark night, I let that comment go. It wasn't worth trying to explain the price of mechanics who specialize in foreign-made cars. Besides, he was probably right. Although he'd play hell making me admit it.

For awhile, there was only the cranking grind of the engine and Casey peering intently at the trail ahead. As the car climbed, the lights hurled to a thicket of trees, illuminating a hemlock. Its slender limbs whipped helplessly in the moaning wind.

I shivered and rubbed the goosebumps on my upper arms. "Do you think we're lost? I thought we were going back to the main road. You know, this whole trip was probably not a good idea. Maybe we should turn back."

"Too late. No place to turn around. Soon as we find a level spot up the road here, I'll stop and make camp."

The wheels slammed into something hard and immovable. Probably a boulder. Our heads bumped the car ceiling. I grabbed the dash board with both hands, thoroughly frightened. "This is no road. It's hardly a trail."

Tree limbs snapped on the side of the car, scraping paint. "Can't help it now. Hang in there, Kath. We'll stop as soon as I see a place."

Just ahead, a jag of lightning crackled, toppling a tree directly in front of us. I gasped. "Watch out!" Seconds later, a rumble of thunder stormed across the heavens as if it meant to grab the earth in its fury and shake it like a rat. "Omigod. Casey. Be careful."

"Kathy. Will you calm down? We're not gonna crash."

"Calm down? What do you mean, calm down. I'll be 'calm' when you stop trying to wreck my car." I drew a jagged breath, and as if I'd suddenly thought of it, I said, "Look. If this is what it's going to mean to be married to you, I don't think . . . "

He glared at me, quickly, unable to take his eyes off the trail for long. "And just what's that supposed to mean?" As the car edged around a fallen tree and topped a rise, Casey angrily geared down into first.

I huffed and puffed without answering, scared of what I might say, knowing I'd cry while saying it. A small wooden sign flashed by my side of the window. "Look," I said, turning around. "It says there's a lake. Casey, I want to stop. This is level enough." I spied a flat graveled area and pointed. "Pull over here."

"All right, all right." He braked, the car sliding sideways in the gravel. "There's your damn campsite and you've even got a lake. Now, will you give it a rest?"

"Well, what did you expect? We've practically dropped off the end of the earth, and I'm supposed to be happy about it?" Sniffling, I fumbled through the glove compartment looking for my kleenex's, remembering I'd dropped it on the back seat.

Casey paused, touching his forehead to the steering wheel. "Look. We're both tired and cranky. Let's just . . . get through the night as best we can. No sense being at each other's throats. I'll get the tent up and tomorrow we'll try to find out where we are." He jumped out, slinging wet shirt tails behind him and leaving a sodden spot on the car seat. He'd forgotten to change.

I waited, watching his tall, lank body twist and turn in the car lights. *I shouldn't be so hard on him. He tries so hard. And here I am, Old Super Bitch. Back to eating lemons for a living.*

Within minutes, the tent sprouted like a large, blue mushroom. Another roll of thunder grumbled faintly in the distance. The hard rain had petered out to a light patter.

The car door creaked open. Casey bent down and grinned. "The tent's ready. Put this slicker on so you won't get wet."

"Aren't you sweet! You should have been wearing this, yourself. Casey, you better get some dry clothes on before you catch pneumonia."

"Oh, I'm all right. Go straight to the tent, now. I'll heat some soup on the butane stove."

A sudden crackle of lightning jagged across the sky. I pointed to it. "This is incredible." A chilling thrill raced through me. "Look how the light is mirrored in the lake. Where's my camera? I gotta get a picture of this."

The rain had let up and I was determined to follow through with at least part of my plans. I'd been a 'shutterbug' since grade school and grew up wanting to be a pro. To be able to make a living at it. This camping trip was designed to get me more used to the great outdoors and possibly take home some decent shots.

15

"Kathy? Don't wander off. You better get in the tent."

"Just a minute. I'm gonna get set up for the next time it strikes."

"Kathy. Where you going?"

"I'll be right back." A bar of gravel stretched along the lake shore, backed by a high bank of boulders and hard earth. I set off, looking for a high point. Small waves rippled and lapped inches from my feet. *This perspective's no good. I need to be higher.* A strange, acrid odor drifted by my nose.

As I began to climb, Casey's voice echoed across the lake. "Kathy? You really shouldn't be doing that at night. Did you hear me? Those rocks are slippery."

"I'm coming. Just a minute." I'd brought an Olympus Super Zoom 3000. It was light, easy to carry in a case that looped onto my belt, and could be counted on to take a nice picture. I loaded it with film and arranged it on a large, smooth-topped boulder. Then sat down to wait.

This one's going into the art show at Edmonds.

Even though I'd been waiting for it, the clap of thunder startled me. I fumbled for the shutter button and snapped off five or six frames of the biggest, zig-zagged bolt of lightning I'd ever seen. I wasn't sure, but I thought I had some fairly decent shots.

In my excitement, I didn't see the pebbles. My foot slipped. Instinctively, I thrust out my hand to break the fall, my full weight landing on my wrist. Metal clattered against rock, the camera rolling off the edge. I made a futile grab for it . . . "Damn!"

Wedged between some cold, slimy boulders, I arched my back and moved both arms. Other than my sore shoulder and now the wrist, I didn't seem to be hurt. Something soft under my feet had broken my fall. I kicked at it, wondering what it could be. "What in the world . . . ?" Another flash of light exposed a clump of hair. "Oh, yuk!" Dead flesh felt pulpy under my weight. I shuddered.

An animal. It has to be an animal.

Spooked by the remembered horrors of too many late night movies, I scrambled out of the crevasse as quickly as I dared and over to the edge of the boulder. A torrent of rain drenched me from head to toe. I couldn't see a thing.

At least I rescued my camera. Wrapping the strap around my neck in order to free both hands, I began to feel around for the spot where I had climbed up. When I thought I had found the right place, I began to slide off the rock. Halfway down, the rock sheered off to a solid wall with no footholds for the last few feet.

No problem. I can drop that far. I let go, carelessly expecting to feel the crunch of gravel when I landed. But . . . the beach wasn't there.

I'd missed it by a mile.

Deep and incredibly cold water closed over my head. *The lake . . . I've jumped in the lake.* Glubbing and spitting, I flopped my arms and kicked until I could feel semi-hard mud under my feet. Taking a big breath of air, I tried to scream. "Casey! Help. Help me!" There was no way to tell if it was loud enough.

My legs and arms moved like they were made of lead. The dreadful, numbing cold, dulled my mind. Stealing long moments of consciousness . . . .

I had to climb, to get out. But my body was too heavy.

Tried again to scream. "Casey." It came out more like a squeak.

I must have passed out. A rude blow on my cheek nudged me away from the edge of blackness. My stomach wretched, the upchuck tasting of stale, lake water. "Are you all right?" I slowly became aware of Casey. He'd slapped me on the face. "Talk to me, Kathy. Open your eyes." By pure reflex, I brushed his hand away.

The movement made me cough and I suddenly realized where I was and what had happened to me. Again, I spit. Horrid, shivering spasms cramped my body. I heaved and wheezed, breathing in and out with short, tiny pants.

I fumbled at Casey's shirt, wanting to tell him so many things . . . But the blackness was back, whisking me off to a numbing vacuum.

After awhile, I became conscious of Casey carrying me. He'd cradled my head up under his chin, toting me in both arms like a large doll. I was still shivering, but warmer. He'd wrapped me in his jacket.

In the tent, he dropped my feet to the ground and said, "Can you stand up for a minute?" I nodded. While I'd been rock climbing and trying to drown myself he'd unpacked part of the car.

He snatched a towel from a box of cooking utensils and roughed it through my hair. Then left me to wrap it around my head. A set of sweats were plucked out of my bag and he began to strip my wet clothes off. My snide comment, "Well, don't be shy," was largely ignored. The kerosene lantern glowed in the small

17

space, casting misshapen shadows on the tent wall.

"Didn't I tell you not to wander off?" he grumbled.

I mimicked him, "Didn't I tell you . . . ?"

He stopped undressing me and glared. I held up both hands and said, "Hey. Go ahead and gripe. I deserve it."

"For Chrissakes, Kathy. You scared the bejesus out of me."

Trying hard not to cry, I helped him peel the wet jeans down my legs and nodded. "It scared me too."

"What the hell were you doing?"

"Taking pictures. I know, I know. I should have been more careful. By the way, in case you're interested, there's something dead over there."

He motioned to the towel. "Keep on rubbing. You've got to dry your hair really good." Rummaging through the box of kitchen things, he brought out yet another towel and started on my legs.

Trembling, I looked longingly at the sweatshirt and pants laid out on my sleeping bag. "Jeeze Louise, I'm cold."

Casey picked up the top and motioned for me to raise my arms so he could pull it over my head. "Hypothermia. It's a wonder you ain't dead, yourself." Steadying myself against him, I stepped into the bottoms, already much better.

"Do you got any wool socks?" he asked. Finding them, he pulled them on my feet and unzipped my sleeping bag.

I gratefully crawled in.

"Uh, Casey. There really is something dead over there. I landed on it when I slipped off that rock. That's why I fell in."

"I'll turn this lantern up a bit. See if we can get some heat out of it. Are you getting warmer?"

Wrestling up on one elbow inside the sleeping bag, I resisted the impulse to uncover my arm and shake my finger at him. "See what I mean? You never listen to me." To his blank stare, I said, "I just told you, there's something dead over there. It's the reason why I wasn't looking where I jumped."

Casey bègan stomping the foot pedal on his air pump, forcing little puffs into my air mattress. "What is it, a mouse? There's skunks up here, feeding off the garbage people leave behind."

"I don't know what it is. But it's big and it's dead."

He stopped pumping and cocked his eye at me. "How big would you say it was?"

Now that I had his attention, I could feel my emotions rise

like an upward-bound roller coaster, remembering the fear and the feel of death. I clamped my jaw to keep my teeth from chattering and tried not to look pitiful. "I..uh..I don't know. It was wedged between two rocks when I stepped on it. It's like . . . bigger than a dog. A bear? I don't know. I remember it smelled something awful."

"I'll go check it out," he said, grabbing the flashlight. "Keep drying your hair. I'll be right back."

I must have dozed off the few moments he was gone. The next thing I knew, Casey was standing over me, fidgeting. I was half asleep and had lost interest in the whole idea. But . . . it was I who'd sent him out there. I pried my eyelids open and forced myself to pay attention.

"What kind of bear was it?" I mumbled. "Was it big?"

"Yea. Pretty big. Kathy, I'm sorry about your vacation. But we gotta move out, first thing in the morning."

"Why? Now that we're here, let's see if the storm blows over."

"It ain't the storm, Kathy. Storms don't mean nothing."

I blinked, trying to see him in the false glare of the lantern. He was just standing there. "Casey. I don't like this. What's wrong?"

"Well, I don't mean to scare you, Kathy. But that dead thing you found, wasn't no bear. It's a man. A dead man."

I gasped. "A man! Do you think he fell off that cliff and bonked his head? Maybe he was fishing."

I heard him blow out and saw him flop down on the limp mattress. "I don't think so. Not unless the trout here are armed and dangerous. Kathy, that guy was shot."

Chapter

2

I awoke to the sounds of birds singing and Casey moving around outside the tent. Something was different. Listening carefully, I realized what was missing. The constant patter and drizzle on the tent wall. The rain had stopped.

I stretched my sore, cramped muscles knowing it was time to get up, hating to leave the warm sleeping bag. Finally I got to my feet, using more effort than I would have thought necessary. The tent wall was still wet and sagged inward, reducing the available dry space to a tiny spot in the very center. The suffocating dampness oozed into everything; my clothing, shoes, hair, and threatened to invade my very flesh and bones.

Shivering, I dug into my bags looking for my hiking boots. I was certain I'd packed them. They had to be . . . . *Oh, darn.* They were still on the floor of the trunk. Casey hadn't brought them in yet. In their absence, I stuffed my feet into the thin, canvas shoes I'd worn the day before. I then pulled on an oversized sweater, over the top of my sweats and went outside.

Hunkered in front of a small circle of rocks and nurturing a tiny flame with bark and wood chips, Casey made a sight both primitive and poignant. Instinctively, my hand moved to grab my camera before I remembered having dropped it on the rocks. Hope-

21

fully, Casey found it when he went back. "Did you remember to get my camera?"

He nodded and motioned towards the tent. For a moment, I considered going in after it. But the promising crackle of heat and the first scent of morning coffee lured me to his side. Moving to escape an eye-stinging puff of smoke, I rubbed my hands over the fire to warm them. "Fire feels good," I said, and yawned.

I would have stretched, but a heart-heavy depression threatened to set in each time I thought of that poor dead man, dropped like yesterday's lunch in a wedge of rocks. I'd been bitchy the night before, and in the presence of a grand morning in a great place, I felt I owed a penitence to a Casey and to a man I never met. "Nice morning," I said, to no one and nothing in particular.

"I reckon. Ain't too bad."

"Well. Goodness. The rain's stopped. Is that coffee ready?"

Hefting a long pair of pliers, Casey grasped the handle of the old tin percolator and poured me a cup. "Thanks," I said, drawing strength from the wonderful aroma of Seattle's Best, perked over an open fire. "Smells good, doesn't it? Much better than at home. Must be this mountain air." Casey threw some small branches on the fire, producing an eruption of flying sparks and forcing me to back up. "So. What's next on the agenda? Shouldn't we be packing up so we can go find a sheriff or a ranger station?"

"Reckon we're gonna have to."

Something about his tone was a little odd. Depressing. It had to be the discovery of the dead man and the ruined weekend. Surely, he wasn't still upset over my mouthing off the night before. As I looked at him, I wondered as I had so many times before, what laid behind that long narrow face with its slightly slanted eyes and marvelous cheekbones, that I didn't already know. "Talkative this morning, aren't we?"

He was a little hard to communicate with, this tall stranger who'd recently asked me to marry him. Although we'd met over two years ago, had been dating for most of that and living together for the last eight months, I still felt I had never quite touched his core. He was distant at times, reserved, and prone to sulk when he didn't get his way. This created a problem and the main reason why I had not yet accepted his proposal. Whenever one of my friends would ask me, 'what's he like?' I had a tough time coming up with a credible answer.

22

I poked around in the box of groceries, suddenly feint with the need for food. "What's for breakfast?" Casey reached back and handed me a small foil-wrapped package. "Granola bars? I hate granola bars. They break my teeth."

"There's bacon and eggs if you want. I'll fix it."

"Never mind. There's not time to cook anything." I huddled with him on the log, dunking the granola bar into my second cup of coffee to soften it. A little ways off in the trees, two blue jays squawked, encircled by a flock of noisy crows. Any other time, I would have enjoyed them tremendously.

"It's such a shame we can't stay." I waved an arm to include the mountain, the lake, and all which lay beyond. "In a way, I hate to leave. This is all so perfect." I breathed deeply, feeling a rush I didn't quite understand but knowing it had to do with the thin mountain air, the water, the earth, and the incredible amount of growing things.

After awhile and fortified with my required dosage of caffeine, that old restlessness of mine began to come back. A man lay dead not 30 yards away. I got up and began to pace, growing more and more uncomfortable. "What a dreadful way to die, out here all alone. I think we better pack up and go."

"What's the hurry?"

"Casey, in case you've forgot, there's a dead man over there with his brains blowed all over the rocks."

"'Course I didn't forget. I'm the one who found him," he said, already scraping dirt and gravel with his shoe onto the hot coals. "You thought it was a bear." Having covered the coals with dirt, he then scattered them with his boot and dumped the last of the coffee on top. Grounds and all. "Only thing is, you said yourself, it's nice and peaceful here. We could always just drive down to the ranger station, report it, and then drive back."

"Casey, I don't think we should stay here. Not another minute. Come on, it'll be just as nice at the regular campground." But even as I said it, I knew that was not the case.

It wouldn't be as nice. The state-built campgrounds would be packed with kids, bikes, barking dogs, and everyone of them intent on ruining any decent picture I might try to take.

But besides being spooked, I was also getting more than a little curious. *Who could have killed that man? And why?* "Did you, uh, go over there this morning?"

"Did I go where?"

"You know. Over there." I gestured in the direction of the rocks and the dead body.

"Did I check on that stiff? Sure did. He's still there. Deader'n a doornail. Rain washed most of the blood away."

"Ewe, ick. Casey, there's no need to be gross." I got to my feet and dusted off my behind. "This place is giving me the willies. Let's load up and go."

He agreed.

"Is everything packed?"

"Yep. It's just to load it in the car." Throwing the coffee pot in with the groceries, he hefted the box and propped it under one arm. "You can help by getting the stuff out of the tent so I can take it down. Roll your sleeping bag up real tight and tie it. And check the area to make sure we haven't left anything. Don't forget the granola wrapper."

Outside, Casey was walking the shore line. When I'd finished packing, I joined him. That funny, acrid smell I'd noticed before lingered like a low cloud. While I watched, he scuffed some gravel with his foot and tossed a rock into the lake. He looked up and said, "Ready to go?"

"One more minute. I suppose I could get a couple more pictures while I'm here. Go ahead and warm the car up." While he took the tent down and wadded it into the trunk, I went back to the spot where I'd been the night before.

In the bright light of day, there was a kind of desolate feeling about the lake. A sharp bite to the wind and a white, crusty look to the rocks where the water slapped them. Holding my nose and feeling a tremendous sadness for the man in his rocky grave, I snapped a few pictures of the body. I was sure the sheriff would be grateful to have them.

Casey was in the car, calling me, his voice echoing over the lake's smooth surface. "Kathy?" He was trying to get it started.

"Coming. Just one more."

"Kathy!"

"What? Just a minute." The sheriff would need several close ups of the wound and though much of the blood was gone, there was some still puddled around the body. Behind me, I could hear the starter on the engine growl wearily. I looked up just as Casey slammed out of the drivers seat and opened the car hood. After a moment, he framed his mouth like a megaphone and called. "Kathy. Time to go. Now."

It could have been the wind carrying his voice over the water, but I thought I detected an unusual urgency in his call.

Snapping a few more shots of the body, a chill scampered up my spine, raising the hairs on my neck like tiny flags. I started for the car, scrambling over the rocks. "I'm coming. Don't get your bowels in an uproar."

"No. Don't run!" Like a coach giving signals to an outfielder, Casey leveled his open palms in a gesture to slow down. Walking up to him, I could see he was visibly upset. The car hood was still up. "We gotta get outta here. Now."

"What's wrong?"

"We've been ripped off. All our stuff's gone."

I gasped, a knot of fear tightening in my stomach. "What stuff? What do you mean?"

"Everything that wasn't tied down. All our stuff, except what we put in the tent, is gone. Our boots, backpack, most of the fishing gear, and my rifle. Gone. Somebody stole it out of the car during the night."

"Oh for . . . ," Sheltering my eyes from the sun, I scanned the lake, the mountains, and the road going out. "I can't believe this. Out here in the middle of nowhere, at night, and someone steals our things?"

"Looks like it. And that's not all." He gestured at some wires, loose and dangling around the engine. "Check it out."

"What's this mess? Casey, what's wrong with my car?"

"That's what WAS a distributor cap. It's been busted and the wire's are all ripped out." He slammed the hood back down.

"How'd that happen? Can you fix it? Where's your tools?"

"They got them, too."

I peered into the front seat and the back, unable to believe my own eyes. It was empty. Swept clean, as if it had gone through a car wash with the doors open.

"What're we going to do?"

"Shhh. Be quiet. Whoever did this could still be hanging around." He fumbled with his jacket, zipping it up under his chin.

"You mean . . . the same ones who killed that man out there?"

"Yep. Had to be the murderer. They know we've seen them.

25

Probably watching us now." Standing inside the open car door, his eyes swept the hillsides around us, while stuffing his pockets with the last of the granola bars. "Let's get outta here."

"How? We've got no wheels. Remember?."

"Get away from this car, for one thing." He paused, his gaze glued to a spot on the hill behind us. "Uh, oh." He then purposely turned his back, leaned on the car roof, and said in a tense whisper, "Kath, I want you to start walking toward those trees."

He nodded in the opposite direction of where he'd been staring. "Act like you're going to take some pictures. Take your camera."

"What's wrong? What were you looking at?"

"Never mind. Just walk over to those trees." He nodded in the direction of a large stand of pine trees. "I'll be right behind you."

I gaped at him, hoping that what I thought he meant, he didn't really mean.

"Kath, I said to go. Now, dammit."

"All right. I'm going." Shivers scampered across my shoulders as I walked steadily towards the hillside, listening to every sound in the forest, trying to filter out that which might be made by man. I turned to see if he was coming, but instead, saw him crouched beneath the car. "Aren't you coming?"

"Go on! Keep going!"

"What're you doing?"

He hollered from beneath the car. "Kathleen! Will you just go? I'll be there in a minute."

I hurried on, keeping the car in the corner of my vision. Casey seemed to be hiding underneath it. Suddenly, he popped out and with his long, reaching strides, started after me.

Panic gripped me. I started running.

He shouted to me, "NO. Don't run." Then, he was beside me, his long legs covering twice the distance as mine. "That's it. Just walk."

A dust puff erupted in the dirt a few feet away. A half-second later, a loud, distant pop echoed across the lake. "Okay! Now run for it. Head for those trees!" He grabbed my hand and pulled. I almost tripped, trying to keep up.

Something zinged close to my left ear and a rock shattered, stinging my face with flying particles. Running full out, we scrambled around some scrubby bushes and up a gravely bank.

26

We reached a grove of alder trees and Casey pushed me down behind a fallen log. "Get down." From there, we crawled behind a mound of blackberry bushes. "Okay. Stay here, and don't move."

Panting from the short run and the gripping fright, I reached for Casey. "Hold me. I'm so scared."

"It's all right. We're safe. For now, anyway."

"Was that . . . were they . . . ?"

He nodded in the direction of the hill on the opposite side of the lake. "There's some guys pulling off a few rounds from up there on a knoll. Too far away for a decent shot." We waited, listening . . . .but didn't hear any more guns firing. "Come on. Keep your head down and crawl along behind me." I started after him in a low crouch. "No," he said. "You gotta stay low. On your knees. We can't take any chances. They could spot you through the telescopic lens on their rifles."

We crawled for another 20 feet, the rocks digging into my knees, blackberry vines scraping my arms and catching my hair. "How long do we have to do this?" I winced at a particularly painful gouge to the cheek.

He stopped in a tiny clearing between two pine trees. "This is far enough. You okay?"

I crawled up next to him and fell across his lap. "I guess so."

"Keep your voice down. You'd be surprised how far it carries. Even in the trees."

I sat up and pulled my mop of kinky blond curls away from my face, wishing I had a barrette with which to fasten them down. "I was so scared. I'm still scared."

What's next to fall from the skies? A bomb? A full air raid? A tornado?

"We can stay here until dark."

"And then what? Can't we just leave? Run down to the main road?"

"You wouldn't get a mile in those city shoes. Besides, that's what they expect us to do. They'll be watching the road . . . their snipers ready to pick us off. No, other than that one guy taking an occasional pot shot, trying to frighten us out in the open, I think we're fairly safe in here. Let's wait till dark."

"We can't do anything in the dark. There's no lights . . . nothing."

"S' all right. Don't need to see that much. Means they can't see us, either." He paused, as if in deep thought. "I shoved the ice chest under the car and pulled the plug on the gas tank. That sniper was above me and I don't think he could see that part of the car. I'll go back after dark and start a fire on the shoreline with the gas. Sort of slop it on some of those dead trees. With any luck at all, one of those ranger planes will spot it. They patrol here all the time on the lookout for forest fires."

"I still think we ought to leave."

Gazing into the treetops as if he were looking for something, Casey shook his head, "I'm telling you, Kathy. We won't get past their rifles. Besides, they don't seem to be in any hurry to do anything else. Otherwise, they could have killed us in our sleep. I don't know why, but I think they're concentrating on the road - keeping us up here, stranded, and everyone else out. Probably biding their time until they catch us out in the open."

He reached up and cut a small branch from one of the alders. I couldn't help but ask, "What's that for?"

"I'm gonna whittle this down and make a spear. While the snipers are out there on the road, I'm gonna check out the lake and see if I can latch onto a fish. We got all day to wait until dark and we're going to need some food."

"Oh, give me a break! You're going fishing? Now?"

"Sure. You spear them, just like the Indians used to. Come on," he said, pulling me up and dusting me off. "Let's walk down through the gully."

"What if they see us?"

"Can't," he said, already walking away. "We'll move over to the other end of the lake, around the hill behind them."

"I still think it's a dumb idea," I replied, trying to catch up. "We're running for our lives, Casey. I think we should hide out and wait until we get a chance to beat our hasty retreat."

"What happens if they don't give us that chance?" He walked on, mumbling, and causing me to hurry and catch up so that I could hear the rest. "I'd guess, that's just what they're expecting us to do. Most tenderfoots would. Don't want to make it too easy for them, Kath."

The path curved through a rock-cluttered gully then rose up the other side. I tried to be quiet and not cry out each time my ankle grazed something sharp, but it was tough. Suddenly I slipped,

28

tumbling back down the gully and landing a little too hard. "Damn it, anyway," I said, under my breath, hating the thought that I was completely out of my element. "There goes my shoe and I think I hurt my foot." A painful lump bulged just above my toes. "Why in the hell would anyone steal a person's boots, right out here in the boonies?"

Casey squatted down in front of me and pulled off my shoe. "Don't know, Kath. But you better believe they will do it. That and a whole lot more. From what I seen so far, these guys are some purdy tough customers. Capable of anything." Taking my foot carefully in his hands, he rubbed it. "They shot that one guy in the head. Cold blooded murder. I seen the powder burns." He put the remains of my shoe back on. "Does that feel better?"

"A little bit. Uhm, uh . . . Casey?"

"Yea?"

"Do you think they're going to come after us?"

He shrugged, looking at me closely. "I don't know, Honey. Could be."

I tried not to cry. "What're we going to do?"

"We're gonna do whatever we have to do, to get outta here." Casey patted my ankle. "Now, c'mon. I don't think its broken. Try standing up."

I tested my foot on the hard earth, wincing at the slow ache. "It's not too bad."

"Probably just a sprain." Casey ripped a swatch off the bottom of his shirt. "Let's tie this around your whole foot, shoe and all."

I tried standing again, carefully leaning my whole weight, testing it to see just how bad the ache would be.

"Can you walk on it?"

I nodded. "It's better."

"Come on, then. It's best they don't know exactly where we are."

"Are you sure that guy can't see us?"

Casey grasped the low branch of a pine tree and peered around it. "Yea. I'm sure. The ledge he was shooting from is over on the other side of that hill. There's half a mountain and a tall stand of timber between us and him. Besides, they're going to think we're hightailing it down the road. Wouldn't doubt but what they got another guy setting down there in a blind, waiting to pick us off."

We walked another fifty yards. Finally, the trail led to the edge of the trees. A medium-high bank opened up to a wide stretch of the lake. Casey motioned to me to stay back. "Hold up." He crawled out onto the ledge and looked down at the water.

"What are you doing?"

"Shhht. Your voice carries something awful."

"Well, excuse me," I said, whispering more to myself than him and resolving to spend the rest of the day with my mouth shut. But after a few minutes of watching him stir the lake water with his spear, I couldn't stand it any longer. "What are you looking at?"

"I don't know. There's just something . . . "

I leaned over the side next to him. "Something what?" It looked like water to me. Cold, clear, lake water. I tossed in a small pebble, watched its graceful drop to the bottom. "What did you find?"

It took him a full, agonizing minute to speak. Usually, I tried to give him all the time he needed to ponder and brood. Would even walk away, forgetting I'd ever asked. Then suddenly, hours later, he'd come up to me with a terribly grave expression, surprising me with his fully thought-out theory which, at times, included a philosophy of all humankind.

But today, I was simply in no mood for it. I was scared, cold, and very tempted to kick him into the glacial deep for not answering a simple question.

Finally, he said, "Stay here. I'm going down." He then jumped and slid out of my sight and, I supposed, down to the beach.

I waited that time, a good five minutes. Then, again, I quietly called him. "Casey? What do you see?" My impatience was almost more than my anxiety. But not quite. "What is it? Did you find anything?"

Finally, with the sounds of gravel sliding and rocks plunking into the water, he scrambled up over the top of the bank.

"Migod, Casey. Didn't anyone ever teach you to speak when spoken to? Who or what did you think I was talking to?"

"It's all right, Kath. Calm down, now. There's no need to let them know where we are."

"Well, there are times I could . . . .you make me so darn mad."

He reached over and hugged me. "I had to check out the lake."

"Did you get any fish?"

"Uh . . . no. I didn't."

"Why not? Casey, what's going on? Is there something wrong?"

"Wrong?"

"Yes, wrong." I grabbed the front of his shirt and pulled his head down, forcing him to look at me. "Tell me, Casey. Damn it. I want to know."

"Hey. Just chill out, will ya?" He squinted and gazed out at the lake. "It's . . . weird. There's . . ." Then, with a sad shake of his head, he said, "There ain't nothing there, Kath. I haven't seen a duck since we got here, no water beetles, not even any algae. You look down there and that water's just as clean . . . lake bottom looks like its been scrubbed, except for this white, crusty stuff built up along the edge. Beach looks like its made outta that washed rock you get from a gravel pit."

"Maybe it's a man-made lake."

"I thought of that. But I don't think so."

"Why not?"

"There's plenty of sources for fresh water. Springs, melted snow . . . " He pointed to a wet spot on the bank. "And a small creek over there. No. It's a natural valley. That ain't the problem. Kath, there's no growing things in or right up next to the lake. No swamp grass, no moss . . . there's deer and elk all over these mountains. Bears. Chipmunks. And they outta be coming here to drink. But they ain't. There's no animal signs on the beach, anywhere. Not a single hoof or paw print. None. At all."

"And, I suppose, that includes the fish."

"Well, Kath. Fish can't live with nothing to feed on."

"It's a little tough for humans, too."

"Yea. I know." He pointed to the pine tree above us. "See that? How it's all brown? The trees along the bank should be the greenest ones. And they're not. They're dead or dying, too."

We sat for awhile in the strange silence and ate the last two granola bars. I watched him scratch the two-day stubble on his chin then patted his arm in mute apology for my temper tantrum. "So. What do we do now?"

He exhaled, and said, "That's a good question."

"Don't you have any ideas? I mean . . ." I threw up my hands in exasperation. "Gawd, Casey. We've got no food to speak of, no shoes . . . What are we going to do?"

"Well, first we'll hide farther back in the trees. Wait there till

31

tonight. And, just see what happens. Play it by ear."

"By ear? Our lives are hanging by a thread and you want to play it by ear? We've got to plan. To get organized."

"Look," he said, grasping my shoulder. "There's nothing to plan. Not until we know more about what we're dealing with. Kath, just sit tight. Keep your voice down and wait until dark. And don't be drinking that water. I don't trust it."

"No food, or water either? You really think it's that bad?"

"Yea, I do. It's that bad. At least, wait until I figure out what's happening. There's something bad coming down, here. I don't know what anybody's done, or how it happened, but I swear Kathy. That lake's been poisoned."

Chapter

3

A wild shriek echoed in the trees and startled me awake. I jumped and scrambled to my knees, staring wild-eyed into the dark night. "What's that?"

"It's just a screech owl, looking for his supper. He won't bother us any."

"Well, your owl just scared the life out of me. I thought you said there weren't any animals around here."

"There's some back in here. Once we get away from that lake."

I shuddered and stood up. My butt and the backs of my legs were cold and half numb from the damp ground. "What time is it, anyway? I forgot my watch in the car."

"Well, let's see. Moon's pretty high, I'd guess it to be around midnight. Time for me to go."

"Go? Go where? You didn't tell me you were going."

"I'm going to the car and get some of our stuff." He gave me a one-armed hug and plopped a kiss on my forehead. "You stay here."

I hugged him back, enjoying his warmth and his concern. "Lord, it'd sure be nice to have my heavy coat. This blazer from work just doesn't do it out here on the damp ground. And the sleeping bags . . . and FOOD, Casey. Bring us some real food."

"I'll try. Stay here and keep quiet."

I watched him walk away, disappearing in the gloomy dark. I'd been ordered to wait here for him to come back.

Forget that shit.

I decided to follow him. Four steps later, I tripped over a log. "Damn it! Oh, great. This is just great!"

"What're you doing? I told you to stay back."

"I heard you. Damn it, Casey. I hate these woods in the dark and I'm not going to sit here, by myself, while you wander around like some kind of a caveman." I sat down on the log, choked back a sudden sob and gingerly touched the sore spot on my leg. "So stop telling me to stay back and do something. It hurts."

"Let me see." He bent over my foot and lightly kneaded the swollen part. "Did you sprain your ankle again? See if you can stand."

"No, I don't think its sprained. This time, its my leg and it burns like hell. Am I bleeding?"

"It's just scraped. You're all right," he said, as he pulled me up.

"I feel like such a goof," I said, leaning against him and enjoying the feel of his sinewy strength and his warmth. "I've got to be the clumsiest woman alive."

"Could be. But you're also the cutest. You and your pretty brown eyes."

"How can you tell? It's so dark . . . ,"

He kissed me on the lips, a quick but warm smooch. "You know, the reason I wanted you to stay here was so you wouldn't get hurt. Why don't you sit down on the log and wait for me?"

"I can't."

"What do you mean, you can't? Of course you can. Just sit down. It's right there behind you."

"I know where the log is, Casey. That's not what I meant."

"Then what is it, Kathy?"

"I already told you. I'm not going to sit here, in the dark, with a wild creatures lurking about and licking their chops. Waiting for a chance to pounce on my bones."

"Nothing's going to hurt you."

"Then why are you leaving?"

"I'm not leaving. Just trying to take care of things, that's all. And you. I gotta take care of you, don't I?"

"I guess so. Somebody has to. I keep getting attacked by these trees."

"Don't be scared. Sit down on the log and stay there. I'll be right back."

"Who said I was scared? I never said I was scared. Spooked, maybe. Just spooked. It's not the same as scared."

"All right. You're not scared."

"Right."

"And you're not staying here."

"You got it."

Casey paused to take a deep breath. In the faint moonlight trickling through the treetops, I could see him lay his head back in exasperation. "Come on, then. But stick close. Once we get out of the trees, you can't make a sound. OK? Not a word. If I start to run and you can't keep up, just duck down behind something. And wait until I come back for you."

"Ok. I'll keep up. I promise."

We crept up the same trail, taking the better part of an hour. Suddenly, Casey crouched down behind a clump of bushes and motioned to me to do the same. "All right now, this is the edge of the trees." I barely saw the outline of his arm as he swung it to point. "Car's over there. Keep your head down and we'll make a run for it. Stay behind me and do exactly as I do. And for Chrissakes, be quiet!"

Scraps of moonlight caught the dull glint of my old Porsche. It looked abandoned and as out of its element as I felt. Beyond it, the lake lapped at the shoreline. A slight breeze wafted by, carrying that same soapy, caustic smell.

He turned to look closely at my face, obviously hoping I'd want to stay put, and whispered hoarsely, "Are you sure . . .?"

"I'm sure."

"Ready then?"

I nodded.

From his crouched position, he said, "First we fetch the ice chest from under the car and pour it on those logs down by the water. Then, if there's still time, we'll get what stuff there is out of the back seat." He paused while we both listened intently. Then stood up. "Let's go."

We ran, swiftly and silently over the path and reached the car within minutes. No sounds broke the stillness, other than our feet hitting the hard earth and our frightened breathing. Casey slid under the car, head first, and started tugging on the metal ice chest.

While he wiggled and grunted in the gravel, I noticed something on the other side of the log where we'd pitched our tent the night before. I heard metal scrape against rock and Casey calling me from under the car. "Take the other handle."

"Where's the lid?"

"How do I know. Will you quit goofing off and help me with this thing?"

Obviously, if we were to slop gas all the way from the car to the log and then light it, the Porsche would also go up in flames. I called back, keeping it to a hoarse whisper. "Just a minute."

"Wait. I need you to pull on this thing. I can't get it out this way. Kathy? Kathy! Where are you?"

I couldn't get what I wanted without taking a chance on being seen. I deliberated for about three seconds. "Just a minute. I'll be right back."

"For Chrissakes, Kath! Come on. If they see us, we're dead meat."

Five seconds later, I had made my mad dash, out and back. "Then be quiet, yourself. I'm right here. What do you want?"

"I want you to help me carry this ice chest. It's full all the way to the top and the gas is going all over the place." Casey wiggled out from under the car, pulling the chest with one hand.

The lid had been dropped next to the front wheel. "Then put this on it. Here." I picked it up and positioned it on top of the chest, snapping the metal hooks in place. "Now it won't spill."

"Help me carry it over to those dead trees by the water. Easy, now. I don't want to set the car on fire, too."

The car window was down, giving me a glimpse of the back seat. I quickly opened the door . . . heard its rusty screetch. Casey freaked. "Kathy! Quit goofing off. You dumb broad! What are you doing now?"

I got what I wanted and closed the door as quickly as I could. "Well, I'll tell you what I'm not," I said, keeping my voice low, my nails digging into the opposite handle from his. "I'm not dumb, I'm not a broad, and I'm not shouting. Now shut up and let's get this over with."

"Easy, easy. Over to the shoreline . . . there. Now, pick it up and dribble a little on this log. That's it." A loud pop careened across the lake and I heard something like the buzz of a bee zinging over the top of my head. "What was that?"

"They're shooting at us. C'mon." I started to set my end of the chest down, but Casey stopped me, and snapped the lid back in place. "No. We'll take the chest with us. Just run for the trees. Hurry."

I ran up the path, the small sticks and pine cones sticking in my feet through the holes in my shoes. The bullets from their guns gouged small puffs in the dirt around us, seconds before the sounds of the rifle echoed across the lake. Casey was in the lead, pulling me along with the ice chest.

"Get down," he whispered. We knelt behind the same group of alder trees we'd been in before. "Quick. Before they see you."

I did as he said. The old log crumbled under my knees when I knelt on it. It smelled rotten.

"Set it in there," he ordered. "Inside the log." He struggled with the metal chest, squeaking it into the far end of the hole. "Now you. C'mon, Kate. Scoot in there. Hurry."

"Uck! There's bugs in here."

"They won't hurt you. Move!"

I got in the tiny space, squirreled up next to the chest. Something crawled across my scalp. I stifled a scream, started scrambling back out. Immediately, Casey shoved down on the top of my head, whispering hoarsely, "No. Stay in there. I can see the guy with the rifle. He's down by the car."

"But, there's spiders . . ." Afraid to come out and afraid to stay in there, I trembled violently, waiting . . ."Casey?"

"Shut up. Here he comes."

More waiting, my insides vibrating with panic. Casey had disappeared. My ears strained to hear any unfamiliar sounds; a footstep, an uncommon rustle in the leaves, a click of a rifle reloading . . . . My imagination was on override, wild with visions of hiking boots, suddenly ripping into my log. Big, hairy hands dragging me out into the dreaded night. Clawing, raping, killing . . .

Suddenly, it was there. A shoe crunched dirt and pieces of log just inches from my hiding place. Someone was breathing, panting, an invading hand reached in.

I kicked. Hard as I could, felt the scrape of my flimsy sole against his shin. "No. Stop it," I cried. "Leave me alone."

"Ouch. Kate! Don't kick. It's me."

"Casey? What are you doing? You scared me."

"C'mon out. Whoever it was, is gone."

I rolled out onto the ground, scratching bugs and dirt out of my hair, brushing them off my clothes.

"Damn," Casey remarked, "You really got me." He was rubbing his leg where I'd kicked him, his voice softening with humor. "You swing a mean leg, Lady."

"Well? You shouldn't come up on me like that. How was I supposed to know it was you?"

Casey didn't answer that one, either. He was looking in the direction of the road when I realized I'd been listening to a faint sound in the distance. "Is that what I think it is?"

"Yup. I hear it."

"How about that? It's a truck! Casey, there's a truck coming."

4

We ran to the edge of the road, waiting for the truck to approach. Within minutes, wide lights swept from side to side as the truck twisted up the narrow turns. A separate light on the side probed the woods as they passed. Casey grasped my arm and pulled me behind a large tree trunk. "You stay here, out of sight. I'll go flag him down."

"No! Wait. What if they're the wrong . . . "

Too late. In a few long strides, Casey reached the edge of the bank and started sliding down. "Hello. There in the truck," he called. "Yeo!" He then jumped in front of the truck lights.

The truck geared down and stopped. Casey waved both arms over his head as the truck lights cast his shadow in long, snakelike patterns on the rocky gravel. "We're campers. Stranded out here with no car. How about a ride?"

As I watched the road, a small black and silent shape flew just inches from my face. The chilling air from its flapping wings raised my neck hairs to full mast. God only knew what the creature was, but I had no intentions of staying here with it.

I ran after Casey.

By the time I got to the edge of the trees, the truck had stopped and a second man in the passenger seat was rolling down his window. I heard a metallic clunk of metal against glass, saw him point a black tubular shape toward Casey.

What is . . . Ohmigod. He's got a gun.

Casey was still in the road, his hand cupping his eyes, staring back at the blinding lights. As I watched, he began a slow side-step, easing back towards the ditch.

Quickly, I kneeled down out of sight, hiding in the dark shadows of a bush. Neither one of the men in the truck acted as if they had seen me. The man on the passenger side hollered to Casey over the sound of the idling engine, beaming the search light on him with full force. "Don't be making any sudden moves, man. I got you covered, good. You want to come over here, into the headlights?"

Casey took a step back to the center and then another, framed eerily in the truck lights, empty hands thrust to the black sky. "We've been stranded. We need help."

The driver then spoke for the first time. "Move farther, where I can see you.

"Hey. Alls we need is a lift to the Ranger Station. Happy to ride in the back."

I edged closer, trying to get a look at the men in the cab. In my fight against the bugs and mosquitos trying to nest in my hair, I didn't see the bank drop-off. As I fell and tumbled down the dirt bank, Casey bellowed at me. "Kathy, no. Stay back."

That caused the other man in the truck cab to perk up. "Who's that? You got a woman in there?"

I landed in the ditch about 10 feet from Casey. The man with the search light wasted no time in flooding me with its beam.

The cab door creaked open on the passenger side, and the other guy peered out. "Gawd, a-mighty. Ralph? It is a woman. Looks like she's blonde, too."

The driver, recognizable by his growl, said, "Stay in the lights where I can see you. And get your little woman over here."

I realized where I had heard that sound of metallic clinks before. When I was little more than 6 or 7 years old, my father, a career soldier and Viet Nam vet, had decided that my sister and I needed to learn enough about a rifle so that we could load it, unload it, shoot it if necessary, and know how to keep it clean. We had practiced shooting at the local gun club and it was there that I had first heard the click of a gun being cocked. Tonight was the second time and it was coming from inside that truck. "Casey? What's going on?"

"Kathy. Get outta here. Run back to the camp!"

The driver was set on keeping me there. "Hold up. Freeze."

The bank was too high to crawl up and the truck was blocking the road. I had no idea of where to go. "Which camp? You mean the car?"

The gun, now pointed out the driver's window, was swinging from Casey to me and back. "Hold up there. Halt, or I'll shoot."

Casey was gesturing wildly. "No! Not the car. The other camp. Where we slept."

But the guy in the passenger seat didn't like it. "Wait a minute, Ralph. You can't shoot a woman."

"Then get out and grab her before I blow the dumb broad's head off."

I'd taken all I was going to off that truck driver. At the mention of my most hated description for a woman, I reacted with my usual mode of self-expression. "Dumb broad? Hey, you jackass. Watch what you call me." I stumbled up out of the dirt and struck a pose which I hoped would demand respect. I couldn't get over the bank, or hardly make a run for it down the road with the truck lights illuminating my every step. It was the only thing left to do. And besides, he'd really ignited my short fuse.

The one called Ralph slid off the front seat and tried to grab me. I let loose an elbow into his soft belly and kicked him in the leg. "Get your hands off me."

Casey exploded. "Hey, you assholes. Leave her alone." Fists swinging, he leapt onto the man's back and pummeled the side of his head.

The other door opened, the driver ran around the cab. He shoved the rifle into Casey's side. "Lady! If you want to keep your boyfriend alive, come over here where we can see ya!"

Casey took another smack at the guys jaw and screamed as they both hit the ground, "Get OUTTA HERE."

The driver watched them tumble and roll. He'd brought out a small handgun and proceeded to try for a decent shot. I picked up the rock I had stumbled over and came up behind him.

THUNK, the rock splat on his skull like a ripe watermelon.

Casey bashed the other guy one last time. The guy kicked a bit and wobbled, but he wasn't hardly getting up. Casey then grabbed me and half-threw, half-pushed me back up the bank. "Hurry," he grunted.

I landed on the top of the bank on the side of my sore ankle. "Ouch! Darn it."

Casey was right behind me. He wasted no time in hustling me down the path. After about four steps, I obviously was not going to keep up. He hunched down and motioned to me to climb on piggyback. "Here we go. Grab my neck and hang on."

The truck driver and his friend stumbled around for a minute, looking for a little easier way up. It gave us just enough time for a head start. They were still looking as Casey began a long, reaching trot down the trail.

"Gawd," I said. "I'm such a klutz."

"It's all right. Hang on."

By now, the woods were looking somewhat familiar. I recognized the same old log with the inside rotted out. Casey dumped me alongside, and said, "Crawl inside and keep your voice down."

This time, I remembered not to argue.

"Squeeze up against the ice chest."

"Where are you going?"

"I'll be right up here. I'm going to climb the tree just above you."

No more than five minutes later, the truck driver and his pal had begun to close in on us. I could hear them wheezing from their short run. One of them mumbled to the other, "Do you see 'em anywhere?"

"No. Boss is gonna be mad if we lose 'em."

"Check out that log over there."

Something wiggly and scratchy crawled out of the rotted log and onto my neck. It was headed down my shirt. I swallowed a shriek and bit into the edge of my hand.

This is it. If these guys don't kill us first, I'm going to die from a bug bite. Eaten alive. Picked to the bone by hoards of flesh-eating insects.

"Where? Which log?"

"Up there. That old cedar." The footsteps were close enough to hear the crunch of dry leaves under their boots.

Then a new, shrill voice pealed out. "Ralph? Larry? Come down here. Hurry up." It seemed to be coming from the road.

"Jeez. She's here."

"Yea. I was afraid of that."

"She's gonna be pissed, man. Really pissed."

"Ralph," she shrieked. "I want you to come down here. And bring Larry with you."

"You heard her, Larry. Come on. Let's go on back."

More footsteps, more leaves swishing. Their voices were fading fast as they hurried to the road. "What're you gonna tell her?"

"What is there to tell her? He never came outta the woods. Tell 'er, we couldn't get him in the lights. He was so damned skittish, we never did get a decent chance to nab 'em." The sound of their scheming continued to fade. I waited for what seemed an hour, was probably closer to ten minutes, listening.

Although it came from some distance away, the night was so still I could hear her haranguing the men and their bumbling apologies. "So. Where are my prisoners?" You lose 'em?"

"No. We couldn't get him to come outta the woods. Never did get a decent shot."

"Yer lying. Ralph? What happened?"

"They run off."

"They? There's more than one?"

"Yep. A woman. Blonde, kinda skinny, early to mid-thirties I'd guess, good-looking little . . ."

"Just answer the questions. Did you lose them?"

"I . . . guess we did. That guy hit the woods, running like a scalded ape. They was gone before we ever got up on the bank. Larry and I was tracking them through the woods when we heard you calling to come back. Doesn't much matter, they ain't going far tonight. No transportation, no vittles, and no boots."

"Get in the truck and drive it to camp. Larry, lie to me again and you're out. And when I shoot, I don't miss."

The truck roared up the road, grinding gears and throwing gravel. I eased my back away from the bugs and rotten wood, waiting and holding my breath. It could be a trick.

Listening intently, I tuned into the swish and stir of the trees around me. The rustle of the wind playing in the leaves, the tiny snap of a twig as a small animal scurried into the night. All woodsy sounds. I poked my head out of the log. "Do you think they're gone?"

"Yea. Come on out."

I eased away from the ice chest, shuddering as one last bug

ran over my hand. Casey helped me out. "Oh, I was so scared. Hold me."

"You're OK. Don't cry."

"Where'd they go?"

"I don't know. Up the hill there somewhere. About where that sniper was taking pot shots at us."

In the cold, night air, the cool breeze had strengthened to almost a full wind. "Casey, I'm cold. They're gone, now. Can't we build a fire?" I handed him the cache I'd retrieved from the floor of my car.

"What's this? Where'd you get these matches?"

"When we went after the ice chest. Remember? You were being rude, and telling me . . . let me see. I believe your words were, among other things we've already discussed, `Kathy. Quit goofing off.' I thought that since you were set on building a bonfire with that gas, some matches just might come in handy."

Casey chuckled and hugged my even tighter. "All right. You made your point." He brushed dirt and wood scraps out of my hair and kissed my forehead. "I guess it wouldn't hurt to have a really small fire. Just enough to brighten things up a little."

As he began gathering small twigs and leaves, I noticed his profile stark against the softer shades of moonlight. "What did you think of that woman showing up?"

"I'm not sure what to think. She couldn't have been in the truck with the other two guys. Ain't really room for three sitting abreast in that cab, for one thing. And I would have seen her."

Brushing the rest of the wood scraps off, I leaned against him and asked, "How far away would you say their camp would be?"

"I don't know. Don't even know where it is, other than it's probably up the hill from here. That's the direction the sniper was shooting from and that's where the truck took off for. I'd guess it to be at least a good eight, ten miles from here."

"Then she couldn't have walked."

"Nope. Too far to walk. Unless she started out pretty early."

"Maybe she's been watching us from the outskirts of our camp. Waiting for these guys to show up."

"Could be." He paused and scratched his two-day stubble.

"What's wrong?" I asked. "You don't think she could have been here?"

"Yea, they could have left someone here, all right," he said, pacing in the small space between the trees. "But . . ."

"But what? Gawd, Casey. Talk to me. I hate it the way you'll start to argue, then just trail off, leaving me hanging. Look. It seems logical enough. Why wouldn't they have left someone on the edge of our camp? Might even have had one of those walkie-talkies. Like a command post. Keeping the other guys updated."

"I ain't arguing. I said it could have been." Again, his maddening pause. "I just don't think so."

"And what mental gyrations, pray tell, have brought you to that conclusion?" *Here I go again.* I blew out, trying to release the anger. *I'm not really mad at him. I'm mad at the situation.*

"Seems to me," he said, "that if they'd have had somebody that close, it would have been the guy with the rifle. As she seems to be the boss, I'm surprised she didn't have one. You heard what she said, didn't you? `When I shoot, I don't miss?' A good a rifleman, or I guess I'm supposed to say 'riflewoman', could have picked us off like ducks on a pond. I don't think she had a gun on her. We're probably lucky she didn't."

Casey was right. *Barf. Why do I always have to put my foot in my mouth? I really should give the guy some credit. Listen and learn.*

I reached inside the log and pulled out the rest of the contraband from the campsite. "Here. Have some."

"Fruit leather? You got food, too? What a woman."

"Sure. I told you I was hungry."

We ripped into the packages like starved mongrels. When we'd both finished, and with a wonderful swash-buckling flair, Casey spread his jacket on the needle-cushioned ground and grinned.

"What are you doing?"

"C'mere, you."

I felt his hands playfully inch up my leg. "Casey, that tickles."

"Sit down. You with your little, round rearend. Right here, on my jacket."

"But . . . there's bugs and little creatures just waiting to crawl all over me."

"They wouldn't dare. C'mon."

I kneeled on the jacket and into his waiting arms. "Well, at least we can stay warm."

Chapter

 5

For the second time that night, I woke up, cold and shivering. The pine needles I'd been laying on had long since been crushed by the weight and had turned my bed into a pin-cushion. Under that, a carpet of moss had sponged dew and dampness from the earth, mixed with the broken needles, and smeared my back with a kind of prickly slime. Casey's jacket had been ground into this mixture and was now wedged between us in a sodden hump.

"Ohhh, uck" I said, stretching. "I hate this." I'd rolled onto my right side, which was now half numb and my hair had become so entangled it was now a convenient roost for anything smaller than a fat chicken.

Casey had been snuggling my backside. "Hunh," he said, rolling over and leaving my only warm spot open to the chilling wind. "What do you want?"

"The man wants to know what I want? Well, for starters, I'll want my waterbed, my bathroom, and breakfast at Tiffany's. What do you mean, what do I want? I WANT to get out of here. I'm cold, my underwear's wet, and there's ants in my arm pits."

Casey sat up and ran a hand over his face. He then checked the time on his watch. Watching me peer at it upside down, he said, "Ten to five. It's morning, anyway. If you're hungry, pick some of those blackberries."

47

"Where?"

"We passed some on the way up here. I'll show you."

Slinking back down the hill, I couldn't get over the feeling that I was sneaking around in someone else's back yard, trying to steal something that didn't belong to me.

At the edge of the woods, Casey gestured with a finger pressed to his lips, "Shhh." He then pointed to a large crop of blackberry bushes above and overlooking the lake. "Stay on this side where you can't be seen, in case there's someone watching from the other hillside."

There they were. A luscious-looking clump of black, shiny berries dangling just out of reach, catching the first glint of early morning sun. It had to be one of the most gorgeous sights I'd ever seen. In a simple kind of covenant between the earth and the sky, they bloomed, they grew and they ripened whether anyone saw them or not, rotting and falling to the ground when no one was there to eat them. Standing, lost in contemplation, I remembered my camera. I pulled it out of the deep coat pockets and snapped a picture, quickly, before I ate my entire bunch in one bite.

As I pushed ever deeper into the mound of vines and berries, an extra long thorn gouged the back of my hand. "They're scratchy," I mumbled, swallowing a big mouthful. "But damn, they're good. Is this what you call `living off the land'?"

"I guess," Casey said, chuckling. "Don't eat the green ones."

The sun was rising, making it easier to see. The lake was still veiled by an early morning haze. From our position up on the hill, it looked like any other lake. Small waves cut across the shimmering surface and lapped gently at the gravel and rocks.
Dry leaves and twigs rattled and crunched when we walked and somewhere, off in the distance, some crows cawed. But in between these occasional sounds, the quiet stillness was almost a thing to be touched and my ears kept wanting to ring to make up for the lack of noise. The sun's rays warmed my back as I moved around the mound to the outside, where the berries were riper and more plentiful.

Suddenly, a man's voice echoed across the lake. "Tie that rope to something. Not a rock, stupid. Run it over to that tree." My tranquility shattered, I reacted first with anger at their rude interruption. Then, almost immediately, fear that I could be seen and possibly shot at, swept through me.

48

My gut wrenched and my heart pounded.

I froze.

I could hear the men, behind me and down the hill no more than 50 feet away. One of them said, "This OK?"

"Yea," the other man answered. "Now lower me down. Careful!"

The truck drivers from last night. I looked over at Casey, my head swiveling as if it were fastened with rusty hinges.

Crouched and ready to spring, he gestured for me to kneel. "Stay down and don't move," he whispered. "They won't see us as long as we hold still. And don't look square at them."

I slowly slumped at the knees, foundering in the blackberries, feeling terribly conspicuous. Casey was motionless, with nothing to hide him from the men but a few swinging vines. As I stared, Casey whispered into my ear, "They're hauling that dead guy outta the rocks. I don't think they saw us, or they'd of said something."

The guy who'd been driving the truck hollered down into the crevice between the rocks. "Do ya got him? Tie that rope around his waist." The other one hollered back, but it was too muffled to understand what he said.

The first man's voice carried up the hill as clear as a bell. "I don't give a damn. Get that rope on him, and get outta there."

Adrenalin coursed through me. I wanted to run as far as I could to get away from these men, their dead bodies and their dead lakes. I whirled, striking out . . . when Casey caught me and pulled me into his chest. "No. Stay still. Wait until they're gone."

My body shook with the need to flee. To escape.

The truck driver shouted, "Hurry up, Larry. This is getting downright spooky."

At the sound of his shouting, I turned back, compelled to watch the slow ascent of the rope. Knowing what was on the end of it. My camera bumped against my chest bone and I automatically unsnapped the lens cover, focusing on the grisly scene below.

As the one called Larry topped the rim of the crevice, his voice became more clear. "All right. Haul him up. And help me outta this damn hole."

As soon as Ralph had pulled him up, Larry rolled to one knee, griping as he dusted his trousers. "Christsakes, he stinks. Makes me sick to mah stomach."

The dead body had been flopped over the edge. The driver stepped back and covered his nose with a white hanky. "Of course he stinks. Been dead going on three days," he said, kicking the corpse over on its back.

Through the zoom lens, I shuddered at the man's face. Having been writhed in rigor mortis, his eyes now stared at an unnamed horror. Sharpening the focus with one finger, I continued to snap the shots. At the mention of his nausea, my own stomach churned, threatening to reject my blackberry breakfast. "Casey", I squeaked.

"I know," Casey said. "I can smell it too."

Keeping my voice down, I said in a barely audible whisper, "Well, I'm glad to hear your nasal passages are in good working order. But that's not what I was going to say."

"What then? What do you want?"

"I have to go to the bathroom."

"Go ahead."

"But . . . gawd, Casey. I can't do it here."

As I looked back, I saw Ralph jerk his head up and stare in our direction. "What's that?" he said. "Did you hear something?"

Casey whispered into my ear, "Shhh. The wind's blowing that way. Don't move, don't make a sound."

The driver eyeballed our hillside. "Where?" he said. "Over there?" His gaze raked across the blackberry mound and into the trees behind us. "I don't see nothing. Come on. Quit stalling and load up that stiff. Let's get going."

The sudden fright pressed my need to relieve myself. I pulled on the front of my jeans, trying to hold things back a little longer. "Oooooooh," I said to Casey, breathing through my gritted teeth.

Casey gave me an exasperated look and mumbled, "They can't see you if you don't get up. But they can hear so you'll have to be quiet. Just drop your drawers and go."

Larry crouched, his big ears almost flapping. "Listen. I heard them voices again. Can't you hear nothing, man?"

"Damn it. I told you to load up that stiff and let's go. Hurry up and do what yer told."

"No way, man. That thing's rotten and I ain't gonna carry it."

The driver snatched Larry's shirt front and growled into his face. "Either carry him or end up the same way he did. What's it gonna be?"

Larry pushed away from him, breaking his grasp. "I thought we were friends."

"We are. We're friends. But I'm in charge here, and I said you was carrying that . . . that corpse. And that's it. Now heave that sucker on yer back and let's get outta here."

As I continued to watch through the zoom lens, I saw Larry stare at his partner, his eyes flicking around like a captured mouse in the bottom of a shoe box. "Damn it all to hell, have it yer way," he finally said. "I'm tired of arguing." He turned his back to the dead man and squatted down. "Put him up here. Christ-a-mighty. I'm a driver, not no damn undertaker."

The driver flopped the body onto Larry's back, the lifeless head wobbling loosely on his shoulder. As they clambered down from the rocks, their path led them along the lake beach and past my car. I could hear Larry still griping. "Carrying a dead body all over the damn county. Damn it, Ralph. At's a hell of a way to make a living."

Unable to wait another minute, I had unzipped my jeans and squatted. "They better be gone," I said to Casey, and noticed he was grinning down at me. I made a face by wrinkling my nose and sticking out my tongue.

He chuckled, becoming even more interested in my 'goings on.'

"Can you see if they're gone?"

"Yea. They're gone. Pretty smart though, if you think about it. Can't prove murder without a corpse."

"Well, uh, I . . . don't suppose you'd have some of that toilet paper . . .?"

"Toilet paper? The lady needs toilet paper. Now, why didn't I think of that? Hmm. I could have picked some up in Seattle before we left. Some of that nice unbleached and unperfumed kind that won't make a big bunch of litter in the woods."

"Okay, okay. Don't rub it in."

He plucked a handful of soft leaves off a nearby bush, and handed them to me. He then, very politely, walked a few yards away and looked off in the direction of the lake. After a minute, he said, "Are you ready?"

"Wait a minute." I said, struggling with my jeans and hurriedly pulling them up. "Do people really do this? I mean, as a vacation? A way to enjoy themselves? I feel like an ill-bred oaf."

I brushed the leaves and dirt from my legs as I walked over to Casey and gave him a one-armed hug. But even though his arms were warm and strong, I could tell his attention was elsewhere.

"Stay here a minute," he said. "I want to check something."

"Now what?" A long pause ensued, with no answer. "Casey, can't we just go? Surely, there's no one waiting down the road, this late. We know where those two went. And the woman. How many more can there be?"

"Just a minute. You know, there's something been bothering me about that dead guy."

"What? What're you looking for?"

"Well, if he wasn't a hiker, and I don't think he was, then who was he? I doubt they'd have need for three guys on that truck." I followed Casey out of the protective shade of the trees, stealthily watching the hills and the road for any sign of the truck drivers. We reached the blood-smeared rocks where the body had lain, my skin tingling, my whole being poised and ready to run.

"Look," Casey said, sloshing into the water. "They forgot how clear this lake water is." About ten feet out, he reached in the chest-high water, snatching something off the lake bottom. "See? These're his boots. For some reason, they got tossed out here in the lake. Must have been the guy that killed him, don't know who else would do it." Casey upended them to let the water pour out of the insides. "New ones, too. Lizard skin."

"Cowboy boots? How could anybody be walking around in cowboy boots, up here? That's crazy."

"Yea. That's what I thought. Heels ain't even run-down."

"This is getting really weird."

"Not really, if you think about it." Grabbing my hand, he started running toward the road. "C'mon. Hurry."

The makeshift get-up on my feet flapped and tore away from the soles of my feet. "What are you looking for?" My bare toes skid in the gravel. "Ouch! Wait!" I hobbled after him. "Ohhh. My poor feet."

"I'm looking for this. See?"

"Oh. Is that . . ."

"Horse droppings. Manure. And see here? Hoof prints. Old ones, too. I'd say, probably been here a week or so. That dead guy came in on a horse. And I'll betcha that's how they hauled him back out. Probably had some horses tied on the other side of the rock pile, out of sight." He strode back to the edge of the lake. "Yep. See here? Fresh prints from little more than an hour ago. That's why we didn't hear them."

"Wouldn't we hear a horse?"

"One or two horses, walking in the woods, won't make that much noise. Especially if they're broke to trail. And I'm willing to bet . . ." He followed the tracks up to the trees lining the road. "See here? This is where they had them tied. Last night. Those there look like they belong to a mule. That's why we didn't hear that woman come in. She was riding horseback too and probably packing in supplies."

"You mean, these are a bunch of cowboys?"

"Yep. Well, the dead guy was. And the woman. That's how they travel so well without being noticed. Don't even need the road. There's deer and elk trails all through these mountains. Come on. You ready?"

"Ready for what?"

"To steal some horses. There's only one way outta here, and that's exactly where we're going. We're gonna ride out."

Chapter

6

W e'd been walking uphill for miles. It seemed I'd been listening to that scuffling plod for hours. My breath was coming in great heaves, making my head feel light and airy. Casey had insisted that I wear the dead man's boots. They were awkward and three sizes too big, but the thick leather offered good protection against the sharp rocks and some support for my sore ankle. We'd stuffed the toes with dry leaves.

We were tramping up the same old logging road the truck had taken the night before. "Hold up," I pleaded. "I didn't exactly sign on to go mountain climbing." And for the umpteenth time, Casey slowed and looked back, waiting for me to catch up. *Pride be damned.* Knowing I'd never keep up if I didn't, I finally hooked my fingers on the back of his belt and allowed him to pull me along.

After another hundred yards, Casey gestured to the top of the hill. "Keep your voice down. We won't know what's on the other side till we get there."

Wheezing, I flopped down on a log on the side of the road. "Are we almost there?"

"I don't know." He paused, listening intently, "Shhh." He whispered. "Hear that?"

I'd been too busy catching my breath. "No. What is it?"

"C'mon," he said with an urgent tone. "We better get off the road." He jumped across the ditch and forged into the trees. I followed him.

We waded through small brush and tree branches for the better part of an hour. Casey was sure he'd heard something. Something that didn't belong in these woods. I was exhausted, mindlessly shadowing his every step. Suddenly, he knelt down behind an upturned tree, it's roots pointing crookedly to the sky.

"Get down," he whispered, and peered through an opening between two of the gnarled roots. "Holy shit. Would you just look at that?"

I obediently flopped to the ground, realizing I'd been hearing the faint hum of machinery for some time. After a few weary heaves, I propped my elbow on a clump of dirt, trying to see through the same hole. "What are they doing?"

"Bulldozing."

"What'd they make such a big hole for? What a mess!"

"I know. Seems pretty damn strange. A dead man, a lake with nothing in it, and now this big, humongous hole in the ground. How in the hell do they get away with this kind of shit?" The pit the machines were making, stretched across the mountain top some two to three city-blocks wide and about a third of that deep.

Beyond it, the sides of a big, aluminum warehouse gleamed in the sun. Casey whistled quietly under his breath and said, "There's that semi-truck that we hailed down the other night." As we watched, one of the truck drivers, I thought I recognized him as the one called Ralph, wheeled a fork lift up a ramp and disappeared into the back door of the truck trailer. Almost immediately, the lift backed out, hefting a wooden platform which held two 50 gallon drums. The driver stacked them against the warehouse wall, adding another row to the other 15 or 20 already there.

Casey swung his arm to include all of them. "I'd love to know what's in them cans." As I took a minute to snap a few more pictures, Casey moved away from the tree roots, saying, "Let's work our way around and check it out."

We eased back into the forest and found a deer trail running somewhat parallel to the edge of the trees. My legs were getting rubbery and my feet slid inside the boots with every step, creating painful blisters. And . . . we needed food.

After another hour's walk, the forest opened up to a meadow.

Suddenly, the sun was directly overhead. Surprisingly hot, it had burned the cold chill from the air and was now concentrating its white-hot rays on our unprotected heads. The trail stretched out before me as I plodded on with a single-minded effort. Raise one foot, look for a spot with no sharp rocks or thorns, and put it in front of the other.

Just ahead of me, Casey stumbled, falling head-first into the brush.

At first, I couldn't think. It took a minute. But as I stood, weaving back and forth, I realized that Casey was down. Sprawled in the brush, and not moving. I heard him wheeze and waited for him to roll over.

He didn't roll.

Swaying above him, fighting to stay conscious, I almost gave in to my wobbly knees, to relieve the weight from my sore feet. It began to overwhelm me. Joining him on the ground would have been the easiest thing I'd ever done.

But, I didn't dare.

Can't go down. Not now. I'll never get back up.

I stumbled over next to him and nudged him in the side with my toe. "Casey," I said. "Get up. You have to get up."

Nothing. Not a wiggle.

"Casey? C'mon. I'm just as tired as you are, if not more. But you can't stay here." I nudged again, a little harder. "Get up."

His panting slowed, sounding more like a snore. I kicked, hard as I could, almost toppling with the effort. "Casey! Get up, I said."

Finally, a moan. I kicked him again, my anger growing.

And as I gazed on poor Casey, my Irish grandmother's determination seemed to swell in me, clearing my head. She had gone through a lot worse than a measly two-day hike and little food in order to give her offspring a better life than she'd had. In 1914, carrying an out-of-wedlock child who would eventually become my mother, Granny had boarded a boat for America just outside of Dublin. She'd been forced to leave her soldier-lover dead and cold in his grave and her beloved Ireland in the throes of a revolution against Britain's rule. Out of the 32 original passengers, after two-and-a half weeks of gut-wrenching seasickness with only a bowl of sour porridge twice a day and an occasional scrap of mouldy cheese, she was one of only 24 survivors to walk, unaided, through the gates of Ellis Island off the coast of New York.

I'd be damned if her namesake, I, Kathleen O'Shaughnessy, would see it all go down the drain, now.

I bent over and shook Casey awake. "C'mon," I told him. "I smell smoke. It's coming from a little cabin. There should be food there. C'mon, Casey. Let's go get some food."

He rolled over, with my help, and cracked an eyelid. "Leave me alone," he said. "I've had it. I'm bushed."

I slapped him again, not as gently as I could have, and jiggled his chin. "I'm going after some food," I said. "Are you coming?"

"What food?" he said, coughing into his fist. "There ain't no food around here."

"Well, there sure isn't any down there on the ground. C'mon. Get on your feet. I think I see something."

I helped him sit up, willing my legs to hold, old granny's grit rising up in me in surprising amounts. Poor Casey didn't have the same history. His eyes kept wanting to roll and he seemed to be losing consciousness. But he pulled back quickly enough when I slapped his cheek. "That's enough," he warned.

Once I had his attention, I pointed in the general direction of the aluminum warehouse just barely visible through the trees. "Over there." Off to the right of it, I had spotted a large log house in the shelter of a few pines. From its roof, a spiral of wood smoke curled towards the heavens, wafting luscious whiffs of food in the wind.

"See that?" I said, forcing Casey to look. "Someone's cooking something. Meat. Or maybe a pie. C'mon, Casey. Let's go get some pie."

He turned toward the smell on all fours, body erect and poised like a bird-dog sniffing its prey. I helped him up and with a renewed vigor, as if even the prospect of nourishment had given us strength, we started out. A little weak-kneed and wobbly, but walking.

My feet were sore and my belly growled. But this time, I was in the lead.

7

W e scrambled down the side of a gully, sliding on our back sides and digging into the bank with our heels. As it seemed to meander in the general direction of the cabin, we hiked along the gravely bottom for awhile. The sharp-sided rocks would have been murder on my feet had it not been for the second-hand boots, and my ankle hurt. But the high, rising sides of the cliff wall would make it hard for us to be spotted. It was warm down there out of the wind, and I felt some of my old vitality return with the sound of the chirping birds.

Up ahead, a sudden clatter of small rocks and the crack of a breaking branch quickened my already pounding pulse. I gasped, and fell back. *Someone's here. They've seen us.* My butt hit hard ground. "Ooof!"

I can't see. I blinked at my assailant through blurred vision, tried to focus. He looked like a brown, wobbly stick. NO, it was two brown, wobbly sticks . . . Legs. That's it. They're legs. Moving, coming towards me. I watched them approach through hazy, horrified eyes. His large brown head and shoulders towered above the stick-legs, and he lifted what looked like a large, wet nose with nostrils the size of teacups. He then snorted, snottily.

Snorted?

Behind me, just then, Casey piped up and said, "Look. It's a horse."

Ohmigod. A horse. At the sound of Casey's voice, the agile animal panicked. It reared up, whinnying, hooves far above our heads. And in a scrabble of rocks and gravel, he clambered up the gully wall.

As quickly as he came, he was gone.

"Sure wish I had a rope," Casey said, watching after it.

Angry at myself for being such a dumb, frightened blonde and at Casey for being such a machomale, I snapped at him. "For what, Cowboy? Oh. Let me guess. You're going to rope the mighty steed and leap upon his back like a wild Indian. You'll then tame him and break him to ride, right here in the canyon."

"Well, yeah. Something like that. But I don't think . . ."

"Oh, give me a break. And help me up."

"And just what do you mean by that? You think I couldn't catch him if I had a rope? You want to make a bet? Huh? C'mon, Kathy. Put your money where your mouth is. Let's make a bet."

"Casey, for Chrissakes, we've got to find a way to get out of this forest and go home. Will you get real for a minute?"

"I am real, Kath. C'mon, now. You been putting me down ever since we left Seattle. All I've heard is bitch, bitch, bitch, and what kind of low-life I am for getting you into this. So tell me. You think I'm a worthless sack of shit that don't know a damn thing about anything and I couldn't catch that horse if I had him in a stall? Huh? Is that it?"

"No, that's not what I said. Will you stop it, Casey? Just stop it."

"Then what are you saying, Kathy? Speak up. What ARE you saying?"

In my effort to squelch a crying jag, I said, in a small wail, hating the tinny sound of it. "I'm sorry, Casey. I don't, I don't mean to be such a nag. It's just that . . . there's nothing to eat or drink, not a phone or taxi in sight, and a murderer's on the loose. I feel so stupid for coming up here in the first place. And I'm scared. OK? I'm damn scared."

Casey blew out and leaned on a large rock. "I know," he said. "I'm scared too. But I have an idea. That horse was tame and in pretty good shape. Probably got out of his corral and he's wandering around loose. I'll bet he belongs to the people in that cabin."

Casey scrambled up the side of the bank, and shielding his eyes as best he could, he stared off in the direction the horse had gone. "C'mon," he said. "There's a trail here. A little easier going. Let's go see if there's anyone home."

It was easier. As we walked through a grove of pine trees, they prickled my face and glued their sharp needles in my hair as we swept the branches aside or ducked under the larger ones. They smelled like my household cleanser, but the shade they gave was a godsend. And under them the forest floor was incredibly soft, having been carpeted with twenty or so years of dried leaves.

We arrived at the clearing much sooner than I expected. To the left was a woodpile, stacked about chin-high and some 40 feet long. To the right, a small shed built out of unpainted plywood, barred with a two-by-four across the door and secured with a huge padlock. Beyond that, and between the fronds of a large cedar, I could just make out the outline of the house. It was hard to keep my bearings, but unless I was totally daffy by now, that big hole and the warehouse should be on our far left.

I was amazed we hadn't gotten completely lost. Casey had brought us around in a half-circle, ending up directly across from the point where we'd first spotted the camp.

"Now what?" I asked Casey. "Do you think there's anyone home?"

"Oh, yeah. You kidding? With that big of a fire going in that cookstove and a whole forest worth of dried wood laying around? Nobody but a damn fool would go off and leave that burning all alone. And something tells me, we ain't dealing with no fools. There's some pretty clever hombres in there."

A cool breeze sent shivers down my back and raised goosebumps on my arms. "It's getting chilly," I said, and rubbed my arms to keep warm.

"S' almost dusk. Going get a lot colder before the night is over." Raising up to see better, Casey pointed off to a small open area. "Look over there. Be careful now, don't stare at them. They'll get spooked. Just look beyond them a little ways, keeping them barely in your line of vision."

Following his instructions, I looked in the direction he was pointing. Two deer were just emerging from a thicket, their long muley ears turning like a cone-shaped radar to take in every sound. "Oh, Casey. Aren't they beautiful? Such dainty little steps, I've never seen them out in the wild like this."

"Sure wish I had me a crossbow right about now. Something quiet. We'd have a supper fit for a king."

"How can you say that?"

"Sshhh. Keep your voice down."

"Well, damn it, Casey. That poor thing never did anything to you. You would kill it? That lovely, timid creature . . ."

Casey spoke with a solid resolve. "If it meant the difference between you and I starving, and I could do it without bringing that whole damn horde on our necks, yes. I would."

I almost let lose with another torrent of temper. But this time, I stopped to think. "Well, maybe you're right. I just hate to hear that kind of talk. It's just that, the idea of us slaying that poor thing and ripping into its little body really makes me ill. It takes us down to the level of whoever killed that cowboy."

Casey looked away, jaw muscles bunched and working. "Survival of the fittest, Kath. There's times in life you got to do things. No matter how much you'd rather not."

We rested there, under the pines, for a good hour or so. It was almost dusk by then, and growing cold. Lost in our own thoughts, we didn't speak or even sit too close.

Finally, Casey got up. "There doesn't seem to be anyone around, except maybe one in the house. Stay here and watch. If anyone comes out, don't move unless you really have to. You're off the trail here, and they won't see you if you hold still and stay quiet. I'm going over to that warehouse and see what I can scrounge." With that and a slight rustle of dried leaves, he was gone into the rapidly approaching night.

I had no idea how long Casey would be gone or even if he'd be beaten, killed, and buried in that big hole they were digging and never get back. It was incredibly lonely out here in the woods and the dark with who-knows-what kind of beast lurking nearby. Gnashing its long fanged teeth over the scent of fresh, human flesh. My scent, and my flesh.

Tuning in to the wood sounds around me, each and every rustle, chirp, and coo, the creak and slam of a wooden door startled me so badly that I lost my footing. I stayed where I fell, crouched and huddled on the forest floor, squeezing my thighs together in fear that my pants had become wet.

From the light inside the house, I could just make out the

shape of a man. He was fast approaching in a direct line towards my hiding place. In another 30 seconds, he'd step on me.

Had he seen me? Heard the arguing between Casey and me? Rooted to the ground, I held my breath and tried to blend into the shadows. There was one large rhodie bush between him and me. Ever closer he marched, 6 feet away, then 4 . . .

Just as I thought my lungs would burst from lack of air, he bent over less than two feet and a few scraggly branches between us and retrieved a tennis ball. As he raised up he scanned the trees and bushes slightly over the top of my head, seemingly to feel the danger of my presence. Seeing nothing but the black night, he then turned and proceeded to the plywood shack. Jiggling the metal clasp, he let the door swing wide and stepped inside.

Now's my chance.

Taking a deep breath, I crept in the direction of the same shack, keeping to the other side of the pine trees, my steps muffled by the ages-old carpet of needles. A light beamed from inside the shack onto the yard. He'd obviously found a flashlight.

What else could be in there? I picked up the 2X4, positioned myself to the side of the door, and waited . . .

There's his head . . . his shoulders . . . WHAP! The board met the meat of his face with a wet smack and a crunch of bone. He crumpled to the ground, dropping the flashlight as it tossed looping rays of light to the tree tops.

I picked it up and propped it, facing out, under my arm. Armed now with enough light to see by and with shaking hands, I stripped his belt off his pants and bound his hands together. His eyes fluttered and he began to twitch.

He's waking up. I'll have to hurry.

Fumbling through the boxes and shelves in the shack, I found a new roll of duct tape. Quickly, I stuffed his mouth with the cellophane wrapping and bit off a length of tape to bind his head and jaws. Taking extra care to secure his wrists together, I turned to his ankles.

Suddenly, his legs jerked and kicked, gripped in a fit of seizures. Blood poured from his nose and his eyes rolled back, the whites staring blindly into the dark.

Oh, gawd. I've killed him. Terrified, I watched for a moment. Helpless. I then snatched the tape and paper out of his mouth and tossed them.

Mouth to mouth recusitation. That's it. I'd have to give him CPR. Although the bleeding had slowed, his entire upper lip was covered with a layer of blood and small bubbles snuffled in and out of the nostrils with his every breath.

On second thought, he seems to be breathing OK. Hating to have to hold him still with my hands, I leaned on the ankles with my knee and began to bind them.

After two or three minutes, the convulsions stopped. Eyeing the house and praying that none of his buddies would decide to join him outside, I dragged my captive into the shack. He appeared to be sleeping. Hopefully, it was his body's way of recovering from the seizure and he would not be going into a coma. I propped him head up in the corner to keep him from choking on his own blood.

There was just enough time for a better appraisal of the shelves. *They had to have stored some type of food in here.* Using the flashlight to rummage through the boxes and doodads my hand bumped a small case of vacuum-sealed goods, then another. I quickly stuffed them inside my shirt and turned to leave.

The guy on the floor was half-awake and vomiting. He rolled a bleary eye up at me and blinked. Wiping his face with a rag, I glared at him with as mean a stare as I could manage and said, "Don't make a sound and you won't be hurt."

"Do you know Sister? It's not my fault."

Sister? I must have hit the guy harder than I thought.

"Never mind. Just keep your mouth shut and go back to sleep. Otherwise, I can't be responsible for what they'll do to you. You understand?"

He nodded, obviously scared silly.

I continued my bluff even though I'd lost heart in the whole idea. "Just be quiet and the worst that will happen to you is a cold night in this shack. And if you promise to cooperate, I'll be back to let you out before I leave. If there's any shooting, just duck down on the floor."

I plucked a coat off a nail on the way out.

Chapter

8

Back at the spot where Casey had demanded that I wait — *so much for His Lordship,* I unloaded my cache and hid most of it in the branches of a large cedar tree next to the pines. Ripping into a Slim Jim package and a box of bacon-flavored crackers, I sat down and waited for Casey.

I didn't wait long.

With little more than the snap of a small twig and the rustle of fir bough against his jeans, Casey emerged from the forest and flopped down next to me. "What's that smell?" he asked, sniffing and groping in my lap. "Slim Jims? What the . . . Where'd you get these?"

"Shh," I warned, and handed him several from the box. "Have some. But be quiet. You're making too much noise."

Jaws working, he tore into several packages with his teeth, gobbling the spicy meat almost unchewed. Having downed about half of what I'd given him, he crammed in a handful of string-cheese lengths, mouth open and mumbling. "Know what? You're all right for city girl. Where'd you find these?"

I, gratefully, was able to keep my eyes on my own dinner. "What would you say to some pork and beans?" I asked, tossing him a can while I kept the other.

"Oh, man. This's a feast!"

"I didn't have time to look for a can opener."

"At's all right. Got one right here on my Swiss army knife. He scrambled up, digging deeply into his jeans pocket, and collided with a tree branch. "Ouch. You say they got food stored outside here somewhere?"

As the graceful leaves shuddered and swayed, I peered out to see if his ruckus had caused us to be discovered. "Sort of. I'll show you where it all came from in a minute. But for now, in the words of a wise and bold frontiersman with whom I just happen to be sharing my booty -- put a sock in it. Before they hear you. We've got maybe another ten minutes, twenty minutes tops, until the crew inside begin to suspect foul play and decide to storm the premises."

"Why's that? Think they'll miss their chow? I hope nobody saw you take it. They didn't did they?" Pause. He ceased munching. "Kathleen? Tell me nobody saw you."

"Something like that. He's a little tied up right now."

Casey knew me better than I thought. I was still shook from seeing the man's blood on my hands and watching him in the throes of a seizure. And underneath the attitude, I was dangerously close to losing it all. The heavy food and exertion had turned my stomach to a quivering mass. Not to mention a possible crying jag. He also knew that if asked a pointed and direct question, I would feel duty-bound to answer. "Kath, look at me. What'd you mean, when you said he was tied up?"

I thumbed in the direction of the shed. "He was on his way out as I was going in. What can I say?" I guiltily made a half-hearted motion, meant to show how the board had met the man's skull. "He's still in there. Tied up. He's . . . all right. Probably have a headache for awhile."

"You really got somebody tied up in that shed? You're shitin' me."

"Do you have any better ideas?"

"No. I'm just surprised is all. That you would do that."

Sniffling and biting back an urge to vomit, I drew up my knees and curled into a ball. "You know, you don't have to be such a poop about it. Maybe I should take the food and drinks back. Let us both die of deprivation."

Casey shook his head and gaped at me with a kind of wonder and new respect. "NO. No, not at all. I didn't mean that. I'm just amazed that you really bashed some guy over the head. I've never known you to do anything like that before. Besides stealing his chow and tying him up. All by yourself."

"Casey. You're making me nervous. Just forget it ever happened, OK? *Thank God the guy's not dead.* Get over it. Besides, any minute now, his buddies are going to realize he's been gone too long. Can't you imagine what they'll think? An empty chair at the Friday night poker game. His turn to bet. `Hey,' they'll say. `Somebody go out and check up on . . . whoever'. When that happens, they're certain to . . ."

"You're right. We got to get outta here. I think there might be some stuff down in that warehouse that might help us, but they got so damn many guards and dogs that . . ."

"Shhh. I hear something . . ."

The cabin door scraped open, and there, framed in the dim light from what was probably a kerosene lamp, a hulky, heavy-shouldered man ambled onto the step. He called out towards the storage shack. "Hey, Bubba. You out there? Sister says you should come in. Bubba?"

Sister? Were they all related?

He, of course, did not receive a reply. Bubba, as I had related to Casey, was all tied up.

Moments later, a sharp, caustic voice from inside the cabin, I couldn't quite make out what she said, seemed to goad the heavy guy. He turned and said something in reply. And although I hadn't understood what he said, I did hear the sound of his voice.

It was somewhat less than pleasant.

This guy's reaction, his whole demeanor, seemed to forebode danger. Even though he didn't necessarily seem to be angry or even worried about the other's disappearance, the whole set-up was a little more than I'd expected.

But, the other voice, I was sure I'd heard before. It belonged to a woman. A woman who, just last night, had sicced a crew of truck drivers on our tail from atop a horse.

Casey was tugging on my arm and whispering wetly into my ear. "Come on, Kath. Let's scoot. Before the guy in the shed gets loose or the rest of them come out, blasting away."

Somehow, I couldn't quite imagine the guy I'd hit as being armed and dangerous. But Casey was right. There was no need to be this close to that house.

I hated the thought of tramping back into the black night. The used boots were way too big and had worn blisters on the sides of my heels. And they were awfully heavy. It was a toss-up as to whether they were worth it. But without them, it meant I was back to the canvas slippers which had been reduced to little more than rags.

Waging war with the elements in broad daylight had been bad enough. Now I'd be searching for a path between razor-edged leaves and needled pines, stumbling over rocks and roots on my sore feet, and all in the dark. Not to mention the bats and the rats and the bears. And even though the pale light from the window yielded a sparse, if any, warmth, it was the only evidence of civilization in this wild land and I'd miss it.

We stuffed our pockets with the last of my loot and I followed Casey down the hill. It was a slow and treacherous hike. The cowboy boots had been left under the bush.

After a few hours of blocking the exhaustion from my mind and willing my cut and bruised feet to take yet another step, and then another, we arrived back at the gully. The clouds had dissolved into thin wisps, exposing a half-round of moon. A biting cold wind gnawed at my cheeks and made knots in the long tendrils of my kinky hair.

Consumed by an overwhelming weariness, I lowered myself onto a rock, frightened by the sense that the ground beneath me was beginning to sway. I leaned back, ready to plunge headlong into a vacuum of swirling black, wondering vaguely, if I would ever come back . . .

"I'll be damned."

Casey. There he goes, again. Spouting colloquialisms.

"Look at this, Kath."

I'll ignore him. Pretend I'm already asleep.

"Kath? Look. We're saved."

Casey's voice was sounding farther and farther away. *He's working on my curiosity. Just like a man. Thinks he can make me wake up.* I was beginning to feel warmer, almost starting to float . . .

"Kath? Look at this. We're gonna be all right. Kath? Hey. Wake up."

I hate it when he does that. Knows I'll start wondering . . .

"Hey. You gotta see this."

"Damn it all to hell, Casey. Would you just stop? What is it?"

"It's another horse, Dingbat. Half-starved. Its saddle's all tangled in the brush. And a pack mule. Hey. There's food here, a tent, sleeping bags, Kath? Come look at this. We got a friggin' store tied to the back of this mule."

Angry and too tired to be rational, I folded my arms and squeezed my eyes shut. "Fine. You've got a hungry horse. I can relate to that. Now can I sleep?"

"Come on," he said, picking me up and half dragging me over to the horse. "Get up on top here and let's go. I think this horse smells water."

Wide awake now, I grasped the saddle horn with both hands. "Casey, am I supposed to ride this thing?"

"Unless you'd prefer to walk and let me ride it."

I must have dozed in the saddle. The horizon was showing a light salmon pink when Casey lifted me to the ground and walked me a few paces upstream. "There's good cold water here. And lots of it. Get yourself a drink. Go ahead. Down on your knees and slurp it right up. That's it. There you go."

He was right. The horse had taken us directly to a small stream where the water was cold, very wet, and absolutely delicious. When I drank all I could for the moment, I thought about getting up. Even made a half-hearted attempt. But my legs would only shake and quiver, refusing to hold me.

He must have been as exhausted as I was, but somehow, he found the strength to make a small fire. Cutting his eyes at me, his jaws bunched with worry, Casey settled a tin coffee pot onto the rocks positioning it directly over the flames, and came to my aid. "Sit over here where it's warm," he said, carrying me up the bank in both arms. "I'll make camp here for tonight. Worry about the rest tomorrow."

He heated some foil-wrapped packages. I'd curled up inside the sleeping bags close enough to the fire to feel the warmth, and ate my supper propped up on one elbow. It was morning before I remembered to tell him he'd done good.

And by then, it was too late.

I awoke with the end of a gun barrel poked into the soft flesh just under my left breast. As close to my wildly beating heart as a bullet could get without the pistol being fired. In my fear, I could

69

barely make out the visage of the man who held it there. All I could see, leering down at me, was a face full of grey whiskers, thin lips which barely moved when he spoke, and a ridiculous plaid wool hat with man-made fur on the inside flaps. He had to repeat his demands twice before I realized I'd best obey him or die.

"Get up," he ordered. "Get up slowly, and don't make a sound."

I looked over and saw another guy, his face hidden behind longish hair and a full black beard, looming over Casey, working the bolt action on some kind of a rifle. The gun was trained on his throat. "Don't even think about it," the guy said, poking Casey's adams apple with the sight on the end of the barrel.

We clambered to our feet, clumsily. At one point, I almost fell, straining the muscles in my legs and back with a piercing groan.

"Now, walk," the guy closest to Casey ordered, pointing upstream with his rifle.

The one next to me repeated his demands. "You too. Get going."

The days upon days of starving and continually pushing our bodies far beyond their limits, must have affected Casey's mind. He balked. "Nope," he said, shaking his head and glowering at his captors. "Can't do it." The two men exchanged glares for a moment, reminding me of two rutting rams I'd seen on some nature show. I began to hope that the bad guys might actually back off.

But the one with the rifle seemed to take it as a personal affront and clearly felt he had to prove himself. "I said to get going. And hurry it up or I'll blow your kneecaps into the next county."

Casey simply shook his head again. "Do what you want with me. But we ain't walking nowhere. My girlfriend's all done in. She won't make it. You want us to go, put her on the horse," he said, motioning to me with a quick jerk of his head and gazing fondly at me for a moment. "She's come as far as she's gonna, with the little food and rest she's had. Pushing her any farther would kill her anyways, and then I'd be bound to come after you. Gun or no gun." After a mind-boggling moment of silence, Casey then added, "You want to send us off to meet our maker, then do it now. Right here, in cold blood and while we're looking you straight in the eye. Otherwise, give us a minute to eat, and see to it that she gets to ride."

9

The one with the whiskers seemed to be more reasonable. "Sounds OK to me. Go ahead and fix yourselves something. Pour me a cup of that coffee while you're at it."

His bearded buddy was less charitable. "You mean, you're going to let them get away with this shit? Telling us what they're going to do and what they ain't?"

Before answering, Whiskers downed a couple gulps of coffee, except for the grounds which had settled on the bottom, and with a disgusted jerk he pitched the empty cup onto the tarp which held the rest of the utensils. "What I'm going to do, is let them eat," he said, between tightly clamped teeth. "This girl does look pretty pale. Get some wood over here and stoke up this fire." Raising his left eyebrow a notch at his partner, he then yanked an extra pair of leather gloves from his pocket and tossed them to Casey. Motioning in my direction, he said, "Wrap these around her feet. Do you have anything that'll cook up right away?"

Casey nodded, quickly scooping up the gloves and moving toward the pack. "I got oatmeal. Instant. All's we gotta do is heat the water."

"That's fine. Go ahead and cook. Don't make any stupid moves that'll get you hurt and we'll all get through this in one piece. Careful, don't put out those hot coals."

We finished eating, Casey fixing a bowl for the man with the grey whiskers. He'd offered the younger one a share, but in a show of wounded pride the guy turned it down, preferring to prop himself against a large rock, stroking his beard to keep the stray hairs out of his mouth, and glaring at Casey from under a big floppy hat. It was a silly-looking thing that reminded me of the one Jed Clampet wore in the Beverly Hillbillies. 'Beard' also kept his rifle aimed at Casey's chest. Once, he even said "Ka-boom" and made a clicking sound with his tongue and cheek as if he were reloading.

Casey gave no sign he'd heard him.

The horse had drank his fill from the creek and was feeding in a sunny meadow about twenty feet away. Casey had removed the saddle and bridle the night before and shackled the animal with a short rope, which left him the ability to hobble from one fresh clump of grass to another, ripping it from its roots in huge hungry bites, but hindering his ability to run. Having reserved a little of the dry cereal in the bottom of his hat, Casey offered it to the muscular bay and quickly snaked the reins from the bridle around his neck.

The horse must have missed, terribly, the man or woman who had trained him. He was definitely a prized pet. With a friendly nicker and an affectionate rub of his head on Casey's arm, the gelding accepted the cold bit, ready and willing for work.

The sun was up and turning warm in a clear sky by the time we were on our way. Casey and I both were on the horse, he in the saddle and I clinging, desperately, to his back. It struck me how I was so very glad he was there to hold onto. That thought was followed by a sting of guilt as to how I'd snapped at him, constantly finding fault, only days before.

How time flies when you're having fun.

Our captors retrieved their horses from some yards away. Laying claim to the mule and the priceless bundle on its back, the one with the whiskers led the way upstream. The other one, with all but his eyes and a slash of thin lip hidden behind the beard, brought up the rear. Rifle still cocked and aimed at our backs.

We climbed most of the day, ascending the side of a hill. Evidently, the trail followed the creek because every now and then I'd hear the splash of water on rock. Occasionally, we'd stop to refill our canteens and let the horses drink. When the trail became too steep or rocky for the horse to surmount with our added weight on its back, we all walked. Casey led the horse with the reins while I literally brought up the rear, hanging on to its tail.

About midday, the horse's sides became frothy with perspired lather and Casey no longer even tried to ride. I sat in the saddle alone, as my weight was not that much of a deterrent. Or so Casey said. Finally, the slope leveled off and we entered what seemed to be a small valley. A small log cabin, its yard, outbuildings and corral stretching over a space the size of a large city block, stood dead ahead.

The horse ambled over to a post and stood to one side of the front porch steps. Since the saddle was already grimy with dirt, pine needles and sloppy horse sweat, my dismount consisted of little more than leaning to one side and letting go of the mantle. I landed on unsteady and incredibly sore legs but with a wet slap to his hind haunches, I bid my trusty steed farewell and tottered up the porch steps.

The door opened to a mid-size living room. I hobbled as far as the first couch and flopped. Beard came in behind me, eyeing my unladylike sprawl. "Kill me if you want," I said. "At this point, you'd simply be putting me out of my misery."

"Who said I was gonna kill you?" His mouth twisted in the depths of his beard. "I never said that. Pretty thing like you? I'd be an awful waste. Naw, I could think of lots of other things to do with you, than that. We don't get too many women up here."

"Really. I never would have guessed."

My thighs were incredibly sore from being stretched across a horse's back. A back that measured a good 30 inches wide. My hips, going straight across, was about half of that. They hadn't been stretched that hard and that far apart since the night of my Senior Prom when I was a 17-year-old virgin about to be deflowered.

I would have preferred to lounge indefinitely, my knees splayed in opposite directions. But I didn't like the way this creep kept darting little hot-eyed squints at my crotch. I squirmed to a more upright position, then gently and using both hands, I crossed my right leg over the left. With all my fun-parts now suitably hidden, Beard's mind moved to another bodily need.

"Don't get too comfortable," he said. "It's time you got yer hiney up to the stove and fixed us some supper."

"Why me? It's your kitchen."

"Time's a-wasting. You'd best be earning yer keep."

I would have argued more forcefully but since it would take more energy than the actual cooking and since a hot meal did sound awfully good, I decided to just do it. It also gave me an excuse to go into another room leaving Beard and his very fragile ego in place.

Getting up was harder and much more painful than sitting down but I managed it. Shaking my head 'no' at his offer of help, I hobbled into the kitchen. I didn't want him that close while I felt so vulnerable.

The stove was cold and there weren't any knobs to turn it on. And other than for one circular cut-out in the iron stove-top, there weren't any burners. Underneath it, nothing but a black hole. Again, I resisted the urge to ask him for help.

Finally, Casey came in with the pack off the mule's back. Whiskers followed closely behind, ever watchful but without making a big show.

"Casey," I whispered, when he'd dumped his load in the corner of the kitchen floor. "That dolt in the other room has demanded that I cook. Damn. I can't use this thing. There's obviously no electricity and I don't see any gas burners. How do you turn it on?"

He chuckled. "You don't. I'll have to build a fire."

"Oh, fine. I'll be cooking on a wood stove. Just call me Grandma Kettle."

Finding everything he needed in a big wooden box on the porch, Casey soon had a fire going in the stove and it was beginning to get hot. "What do I fix? Everything here is so . . ."

"Don't try to fix anything fancy, Hon. I'd just open some cans." He prowled through the cupboards and began to set things down on the counter. "Here. Boil up this package of spaghetti and open a couple jars of sauce. There's green beans, just open them and heat them up a little. And here's some peaches. That ought to do it for tonight."

Beard had entered the doorway and stood watching. Casey eyeballed him and asked, "You got any meat she can cook up quick?"

"Should be some sausage in the smokehouse."

"If you want to fetch it, I believe we can eat in just a little while."

By the time dinner was over, I was bone-weary and ready to stretch out on the table amongst the dirty dishes and be blissfully considered a left-over. Casey had wisely set a teakettle of water on the stove to heat for washing up and it was just beginning to whistle.

I was surprised we had running water. The faucet looked like it belonged outside in a garden, but when turned on, it emitted a stream of extremely cold, running water into a large porcelain basin that served for a sink. Casey and even Whiskers helped with the dishes and it didn't take long to finish.

Two bedrooms sat just off the inside kitchen wall. I stumbled toward them, determined to find something to lie down on. One of the fingers from the leather gloves tied around my feet had worked itself loose. It made a soft slapping sound as I made my way across the kitchen.

"And just where do you think you're going?"

Beard.

I answered him without turning around. "To sleep."

"No you ain't. Not till I say you can."

"Go to hell."

Casey was right behind me. "Keerist," he mumbled. "Is that guy ever going to let up?"

I had a feeling he wouldn't. But I hoped that if Casey and I could only make it as far as a mattress, Old Black Beard would soon tire of his games and let us sleep. I leaped for the closest bedroom, hoping there was a lock on the inside. A surge of urgency sent me scurrying a little too fast. The leather binds on my feet slipped and I stumbled. Scared, I barely managed to roll over and made it up as far as my knees, the leg muscles quivering with exhaustion.

Black Beard knew a moment of weakness when he saw one. Pushing past Casey, he seized one of my feet. "Don't turn your back on me, you bitch. You'll go to bed when and where I say and not a minute sooner."

From pure reflex, I kicked as hard as I could. My glove-shoe came off in his hand and I scrambled on all fours into the bedroom.

He obviously hadn't expected that much resistance. His pause

77

gave Casey time to set his feet, position an elbow, and bash it into the guys jaws. He tumbled back, bellowing and bleeding from a split lip. "I'll get you for that."

Quickly, I scrambled into an open closet, catching a glimpse of Whiskers. He had a choke-hold on Beard and pinned his arm to the back. He saw me watching and said, "Go on to bed, you two. Just don't try to escape and I'll tend to things here."

Seconds before I dozed off, a key rattled in the lock on the bedroom door. Somehow, I doubted that this was the first time this room had held a prisoner. Startled and now wide awake, I turned to Casey and whispered, "Do you have any idea what we're doing here? What in the world is going on with these guys? And why are the locks on the wrong side of the door?"

"Hell, I don't know, Kate. Just have to take things one at a time. I believe we'll probably find out soon enough."

"That's what I'm afraid of."

"Well, we're warm, we've eaten, and been given a bed and blankets. I say, we just go along with whatever the hell they want for now, and see how things take shape in the morning. Try and get some sleep."

The morning took shape about like I thought it would. Whiskers ushered us outside to the outhouse, a smelly two-holer about 10 yards from the house.

Back inside, I was expected to fix breakfast. Not a single 'please', or 'would you mind', but three hungry men with big feet and heavier boots, milling around the kitchen, doing little but getting in the way. But at least the stove had a fire going and seemed to be hot enough. "If you guys will sit down, I'll make a stab at a stack of pancakes."

"There's some pancake mix in the pantry," said Whiskers, clumping across the kitchen, "and I'll go get a ham."

"This smokehouse of yours," I said to no one in particular, "is better than the corner 7-11."

After a few false starts and some gooey wads of half-baked dough in the sink, I managed to 'earn my keep' and feed them.

Is this all they want from me? Their own personal cook and bottlewasher? They could have hired someone to do this. Could my feeble efforts at submitting to forced labor be worth an eventual charge of kidnapping? I don't think so. There's more to this scheme than meets the eye.

78

Casey and I cleaned up under the watchful eye of Black Beard. His rifle, as always, was close at hand. When Whiskers came in from the chores, he looked at Beard and said, "Ready?" The younger man nodded and stood up.

To us, Whiskers said, "We're going to be out for most of today. At least one of us should be back around dinner time. I'm afraid I'll have to tie the both of you up until then." With one hand tightly clamped around my arm, he shoved me into a chair.

I instinctively reacted, pulling away from him and the ropes in his hand. "But, what if something happens? We need a drink. To go to the bathroom. What if you don't come back?"

"That will mean we're either dead or in jail. You better pray that neither of those events occur." He began to lash my hands and feet to the chair.

"You would tell them, wouldn't you? That we're up here? Starving?" He didn't answer. Not even a nod.

Casey's treatment was even worse. Beard thought Casey might untie me if he were tied to a chair that could be scooted around the kitchen. He was ordered to sit on the floor directly in front of an exposed 2X4 in the wall. Threading steel handcuffs behind the supporting beam, they were fastened to each of his wrists. His ankles were tied with yet another rope length.

They left, without a good-bye or a fare-thee-well. And for the first time since we left Seattle, Casey and I were not traipsing through the woods half-starved, or trying to sleep on the open, cold ground. We actually had a chance to talk.

"Well," I said, conversationally. "We wanted to get away from the sidewalks and cement buildings. Although I hadn't planned on this bunch acting as our travel agent."

As usual, Casey didn't answer. Instead, he seemed totally immersed in gloom. And with his dark hair covering the top half of his face, all I could see of him was his full bottom lip. I waited for awhile, hoping he'd feel like talking later on.

We both must have dozed off for several hours. When I awoke, it was late morning and Casey was fidgeting, trying to get comfortable.

"I wonder how long this is going to last," I remarked, hoping Casey would at least acknowledge that I had spoken.

This time, he seemed to have come to some sort of conclusion in his head and was no longer studying his navel. "Probably as long as it takes them to find whatever they're looking for."

"Oh. Well, what do you think that might be?"

"Who knows. Must be something important. At least to them."

"Whatever it is, it has to be connected to that big pit. And the dead cowboy. It'd be too much of a coincidence if it weren't."

"I reckon."

"So, who do you think did it?"

"Huh?"

"Killed that man. The cowboy. Who do you think did it? One of the truck drivers? This black-bearded ape that keeps tying me up? Who do you think?" I never should have asked. It sent him into another five-minute ponder. "And there's that woman," I continued. "We can't forget her."

On that one, Casey all but sprang up from the floor, prevented only by the handcuffs and a heavy supporting wall. "No," he shouted. "There's no way it was her."

"But Casey, how can you be so sure? She is the boss-lady, remember? Bragged about being the best shot in the crowd. She even had the truck drivers a little nervous."

"No, Kathy. That's just not something a woman would do."

"What. Shoot somebody? Don't bet on it."

"I said, NO. And I don't want to talk about it, anymore."

Casey's response had me a little taken back and terribly curious. This time, it was my turn to mull things over. And since I was miffed at him already, I decided to probe a little farther. "By the way, Samantha sends her love. She was out to lunch when you dropped by the office last time, and was disappointed she hadn't seen you." Samantha, or Sam as she's usually called, is the office receptionist and Casey's old girlfriend. Two years ago, he'd been her date at a Christmas party, when he and I had a little too much to drink and decided to open our presents early. The presents being a few indiscretional smooches. Sam found out, raised a ruckus, and had poor Santa having to referee our squabble. The problem was, I was then and still am, her supervisor.

Casey, for some odd reason, had decided long ago he wanted no part of any quarrel between two women. Especially, two women he'd known intimately. He barely grunted at my comment and didn't even glance up.

"Is that place down there keeping you busy?" Casey had been working for a state agency. Evidently, they were a kind of watch-

80

dog for the other state agencies. It never has been made clear just exactly what he did there, or even what the whole agency was meant to do, besides ordering an occasional audit and updating the personnel files. Every now and then, my boss, Darrian, was called by them to perform certain legal duties such as obtaining an injunction or some type of court order.

Casey was still not answering any questions. Of any kind. No response, no theories, and no chit-chat.

I'll try one more time, and that's it. "You know, I've been thinking about leaving the law firm. Find something else that's more fun and not so much pressure."

Bingo. He looked up, and blinked. "Why'd you want do that?"

"I just told you. It's getting too hard to leave my work at the office. The hours are too long, and there's too much stress."

"Well," he said, ponderously. "I hope you think about it, long and hard, before you do something like that. Don't jump into anything you'll be sorry for."

"I've been thinking. I just don't feel the need to study the lint in my bellybutton while doing so."

And with that, he clamped up, braced his back against the post, and proceeded to pretend he was asleep.

I was trying to doze, hoping to make the time go by faster when the kitchen door slammed open. Beard clumped in, his boots tracking mud on the old linoleum. "Well, ain't this a cozy scene," he said. "Reminds me of home. Mamma plunked down at the table shellin' peas or some such thing, and Dad waitin' for us kids to finish the chores." He slid into a chair directly across the table from me and grinned. "Ain't cha happy to see me? I suppose you need untying before you can fix a meal."

"Well, duh. Or maybe I could use kinetic energy and have the pots stir themselves. Are you going to get these ropes off of us or not?"

With a meaty chuckle, he moved around behind me, cursed at the knot on the ropes which had been tied too tight and ended up having to cut them with his knife. The second I was free I headed for the outside door. "Where you going'?" he demanded.

"Keep your pants on. Where do you think? I'm going to the ladies boudoir to powder my nose."

"Just don't try anything stupid. It'd be just like a dumb blonde to run off in the woods and get lost. Remember, I'll be watchin'."

Dumb blonde, huh? Just wait, you little creep.

When I returned, Whiskers sat in the kitchen and Casey had also been untied. A wind had come up and it was dark and cold inside. One of them had lit a few candles and had a fire started in the stove. I went immediately to the pantry and started digging to find something that would feed all these people. A vacuum-sealed container of beef with gravy, a box of instant rice, and a few cans of tomatoes and green peppers would have to do it. Two large cans of créamed corn and I was ready. By the time I had opened everything, the stove seemed to be hot enough to cook on.

I waited until the water was hot enough in the pot before I poured the rice. At first glance, the box the rice was in, appeared to be new and unused. But upon opening the little hole in the side, I found the top had been cleverly sliced along the edge and then taped shut again.

Probably one of those cuts the boxes sometimes get when the stock boys slash the cases open in the grocery stores.

I hadn't measured the water and there was no reason to measure the rice. In trying to determine just how much to add, I dumped a good handful in, stirred for a moment, and then added another. As the box tipped, I felt more than heard a *clunk* on the inside lid.

What in the world . . . I tore the lid off and carefully poured the rest of the rice through my fingers and into the pot. And there in my hand, was a floppy disk. It was an old one of the type those big, clunky computers used when the idea of storing lots of information on a small, portable piece of plastic first became popular.

I quickly palmed it, feeling Beard's eyes on me from the other room. Using all the nonchalance I could muster, I then reached for a worn, white hand towel in the drawer and quickly hid the disk between its folds.

It has to have something to do with these weirdo's. Maybe even the dead cowboy.

Minutes later, while pouring the tomatoes and green chilies on top of the rice which had swelled to an incredible size almost overwhelming its pot, Beard appeared in the doorway. "You about finished cookin'? We're awful damn hungry, here."

"Almost. I'll call you when it's ready." Hoping he'd return to the other room, I made a show of searching the kitchen cupboards for some seasonings and found a can of cayenne pepper in the back of the second shelf. I added several spoonfuls, stirring the burgeoning rice with a long wooden spoon. At the last moment, I discovered a box of ready-mix, stirred up a batch of biscuits, and popped them in the oven.

Load these fools up on carbohydrates and maybe they'll be too groggy to harass me. An opened can of strawberry jam from the pantry completed my cuisine. When they were done and the rice no longer mushroomed under its lid, I called them in to eat. It took them about ten minutes to devour all but a small bowl of rice.

I actually thought I'd be through with these Bozo's until Whiskers propped his elbows on the table, and motioned to Beard and Casey to stay in their seats. I knew what he was doing and I didn't much like it. "Before you start to wash up," he said, looking straight at me. "We're going to have to talk."

"Oh, please. Let me guess. I'm not the chef you had your heart set on and I'm being put on suspension. Either I get it together or I'll have my privileges taken away."

"This has nothing to do with your cooking. It has to do with information. As you've probably guessed by now, we've been waiting for a chance to search the buildings on the compound. Today, we were able to do that but, I'm sorry to say, came away empty-handed."

"Well, I hate to hear that. But we have had nothing to do with any of this. All Casey and I ever wanted, was to get the hell off of this mountain and go home. And if you'd turn us loose, I promise, that's exactly what we would do."

"And you probably would. But, we can't be sure."

"What do you mean, you can't be sure. Sure of what? That I'm completely out of my element and don't belong here?"

"We can't be sure of what you've learned, what you've found, and what you intend to tell the authorities. I'm sorry. It's too risky. I can't let you go." He paused, examining his split finger nails. "The one way we might, is if you tell us everything you know and hand over whatever you found on the dead body of that cowboy."

He's lying. He'd like to turn us lose simply because it'd be easier. But he won't.

Answering quickly, before Casey had a chance to step on his tongue, I said, "We don't know anything about a dead body or a cowboy or anything else, for that matter. All we do know is that our extra clothes, boots, and food were stolen from my car and we hiked up here looking for a ride out."

Beard had a hearty little chuckle over that one. "And your pretty little underthings. Don't forget them."

My new underpants and bikini. "How did you know what I had in that bag?" I gasped. "By God, you're the one who stole them. You've got my boots, you bloody creep. How dare you. Give me my boots back. Now. And my bag."

"You're right. Your gear was stored out in the barn," Whiskers said, and rose from the table. "I'll go get them. I believe your bags and a pair of leather boots were brought inside."

He's full of it. They were left out there while he found time to search through everything. Evidently, my bra and underpants have already been thoroughly pawed over.

Whiskers had no more closed the door behind him, when Beard started in. "Well, whad'ya know. Woman, you done ruined my plans. I had intended to bring 'em to you all along. Maybe tonight. Course, you'd have to model 'em for me when I do." He shook his head and chuckled. "Got to admit, I can't wait to see you in them red see-throughey things. Umm mmm. All that natural blonde hair and red lace. Gets me excited just thinking about it."

I'd never seen Casey truly angry before. Until now. "Keep your hands off her, you son-of-a-bitch."

"And how you gonna stop me? All's I gotta do is tie yer ass up and cart you off. Maybe roll ya down a gully or off a cliff. You sure as hell ain't doing nobody any good around here."

Any minute, the antagonism between Beard and my boyfriend would turn into a full-fledged war.

"Yeh," Casey snarled, "you'd never want to take me on man to man. Back-shootin' bastard. And I'll bet you're the sons-a-bitches that shot at us down there at the lake. Did you ever think for a minute, you were ambushing an unarmed woman?"

"Hey," Beard said. "If you cared about your little woman all that much, why ain't you married her? Huh? Answer me that one, asshole. And don't say ya did, else why ain't she wearing a ring? Great in the sack but not good enough to get tied down. Is that it?"

I could have gladly waited this battle out but I was truly afraid Beard would shoot Casey, just to prove his dominance. "Wait a minute, you two. What am I, cream cheese? Or do I have some say in this matter?" Standing for full effect, I propped my hands on my hips. "Casey, just in case you haven't thought this thing all the way through, I'd like for you to realize that it's not a good idea to pick a fight with a man while he's holding a gun. And you, my dear, are the target." Shifting my attention to Beard, I leveled my right arm at him and pointed. "And you. With the gun. Whether Casey and I are married or not, or intend to do so in the future, is none of your business. Casey and I love each other and I have no plans to admit any other men into my life." Since I'd gotten this far without being shot down or even interrupted, I then waved the arm towards the kitchen. "And just so you'll know, I shall not cook nor clean or even shut up until I get my stuff back. Now, Beard! I'll thank you to fetch our bags, including the boots, thank you very much, and when you get back, you can let Casey go into the pantry and change. I'm going to heat some water and see if I can't wash some of the dirt and stink out of these clothes. And you two can just stop your damn fighting!"

As he began to slink off in the direction he'd been told, Beard chuckled once again. "What was it you called me? Beard?"

"Well, we haven't exactly been formally introduced, now have we? Maybe I could think of something more fitting now that I know you better."

"No. No, that's all right. I kinda like it. Beard," he said, stroking it and eyeing me from under his hillbilly hat. "Hmmm."

Chapter

10

Whiskers was back in the kitchen asking questions while I was scrubbing my jeans in the basin. "You walked up the road to the compound and, presumably, you saw that big two story house.
Did you knock on the door?"

"No. We didn't."

Casey shook his head in agreement.

"Did you talk to anyone? Anyone at all."

"No. No one."

"Why not?"

"Because, someone had been trying to kill us. We hoped to make sure it wasn't them before we popped up like pins in a shooting gallery and said, `Hey. Here we are' and let them blast away at us without having to leave their porch."

"What did you do when you heard the first shots?"

"We hid in the woods."

"How did you make it as far as you did with no food or water or even a pair of shoes?"

"We stumbled a lot. Hey, look," I said, slapping the table with a wet, soapy hand. "This is getting us nowhere. I don't know what you think we're hiding, but I can assure you that all we have done since we left Seattle is try to survive. And it seems we're still trying."

When he grinned, Whisker's upper lip lifted on one side. As if the effort of having to break into a full smile or display any other emotion which might hint of gaiety, was almost more than he could bear. Evidently, my charm and forthright manner had not yet made a suitable impression on the old boy. He didn't like me. "I can assure you, young lady," he said, growing even more angry. "It would not be a good idea to mistake my cordial manner for a lack of resolve. Until that information is found, not one of us, including myself, is leaving this mountaintop. And I dare say, you've noticed that my companion is a man with absolutely no conscience. If I find out that either of you've been lying, I'll sic him on you like a mad dog. That I can promise."

Casey had been quiet as long as he could stand. "Well, what kind of information are you looking for? Books, papers, or what?"

"Computer files. Old ones. They'd be stored on a floppy disk."

Inwardly, at the mention of his search for the disk, I gasped, my heart lurched, and my stomach rolled itself into a tiny little ball. On the outside, I could only hope it didn't show.

"Hell, I couldn't work one of them computers if I had to," Casey said. He happily shook his head in disbelief at the miracles of modern man. "It's all Greek to me."

"Would you recognize one if you saw it?"

"What, a computer? Well, sure. You can't go anywhere anymore without running into some kind of mechanized junk. People typing and stuff. Kate uses one at work and she's got one of her own in her apartment. I seen her use it lots of times."

Shut up you fool. Determined to portray myself as the happy little homemaker, I continued to heat water, wash clothes, and try to decide what to do with all that left-over rice. All the while, in the recesses of my imagination, I was picturing Casey with the gallon or so of rice stuffed, pot and all, into his big mouth.

Whiskers was beginning to take Casey seriously. "How about a floppy disk?" he asked, little squinty eyes darting from Casey to me and back. "Would you recognize one of those if you saw it?"

"Sure. You mean those little plastic jobs? Kate's got a whole box of them, too. Don't ya, Honey?"

"Well, yeah. I mean, doesn't everybody?" I pulled my jeans out of the basin, causing a small wave of soapy water to wet the front of my jogging suit. "Oh, poo. Don't anybody step in this or we'll have mud all over the kitchen."

"Use that towel and wipe it up."

My face was turning red. I couldn't use that towel without him seeing the disk. And that would mean a death sentence for me and Casey both.

His eyes narrowed with distrust. "That one over there."

"It's my last clean one. I'll find something else," I said, heading for the pantry, the priceless package in my grip.

"It's the only small towel in the place."

"You're right," I said, emerging from the tiny room, having quickly relocated my contraband in a large container of corn meal. "I'll just use these old socks." Hot soapy water had done little to the socks I'd been wearing for almost a week but soften the cake of mud on the soles and expose a few holes. I quickly snatched them out of the basin and went to work on the floor. "They'll never come clean, anyway. But at least they won't smell."

That night, I couldn't decide if I should tell Casey about the disk, or not. It would mean he'd be forewarned. It would also mean he'd have to lie if Whiskers put him through another line of questions. I wasn't sure he was fit for the task. Since I'd met Casey, the one thing that attracted me to him with all of our differences was his honesty. He was a very poor liar. Which meant, he hadn't had much practice.

I, on the other hand, could fib, sidestep, fabricate, and speak with forked tongue on demand. And yet I have dared, in the past, to snub this man. I have belittled him for his lack of sophistication and made nasty remarks. Evidently, it had something to do with character. His character, not mine.

The question as to whether or not Casey and I knew where the disk was hidden and could eventually lead them to it, might very well mean that they didn't dare kill us. But the burden of that knowledge would have to be mine and mine alone. As long as there was life in our bodies and limbs, there was the possibility that we could escape, someday.

The next day went about the same. Whiskers and Black Beard stuffed themselves with pancakes, preparing to go out. "Can you fix some extra ones to take with us?"

"Sure. For as long as the pancake mix holds out."

"Sprinkle them with sugar. No margarine. Brown sugar if

you've got enough. Tonight, we'll bring in extra wood and you can bake some bread. For our lunches."

The nerve of these men. Bake them some bread? I don't think so. "Perhaps His Eminence would prefer a nice prune danish at midday and some crispy cherry tarts for high tea."

Beard just loved my brand of humor. His mouth stuffed full of pancake, he snorted a chuckle through his nose. Then, evidently he got a good look at Whiskers' lifted-lip sneer and broke out in a full round of knee-slapping mirth. "C'mon, Doc," Beard said, his stomach merrily bouncing. "Don't be such a hard ass."

Doc? I knew he had been well educated but . . .

"And you shut your mouth."

"Uh, well, I didn't mean that. I mean, you see, he ain't really a doctor, a regular doctor, like you think . . ."

I could not let that one pass without comment. "So. You're a doctor. But not of the type who heals people. Oh, no. This one has them shot. What's that vow doctors are supposed to take? The hippocratic oath. Or is it the hypocritical lie?"

"I said to shut up. Both of you. Or I'll shut you up." He pierced me with a look of pure venom. Moments later, when all was quiet and Beard was passively forking in pancakes, Whiskers directed his attention to Casey. "Could you retrace your steps from the time you got out of your car to the spot where we picked you up?"

"I reckon."

Whisker's chair slid back, the wooden legs scraping a dull screech against the wooden plank floor. "We'll be taking you with us today." He motioned to me. "She can stay here. Alone." To Beard, he said, "Tie her up. And lock that pantry door. She better pray we make it back before she goes mad or dies of hunger."

I was stunned. "You can't leave me all alone like this. Please."

Whiskers squinted at me, his grey eyes the color of clouds on a cold, misty morning. The chilly type of Pacific Northwest morning when I especially hate to get up. "Why not?"

"Well, for one thing, what if I have to go pee?"

"Look, Miss Big-Mouth. You'll be lucky if the worst that happens is that you void all over yourself."

I just had time to refill my coffee cup, slop in some dry milk and sugar and sit it on the table where I'd be able to reach it with my teeth before they slammed me into my chair and tied my hands through the rungs. Casey wrangled an arm loose from Beard and dropped to his knees on the floor beside me. "Don't worry, Sweetie. We'll be back. And I'm gonna get you out of this damn mess, I promise."

Chapter

11

In some ways, this was the toughest part of all. Boredom. No way of overcoming it without moving around or finding an interest of sorts.

To pass the time, I made up dialogue for the bees that buzzed past the window and imagined them as being compelled and driven slaves. Depressed over having to share their one and only woman and make dates with her months in advance. Hundreds of horny workaholics forced to fill their quota of nectar before entering their name on a waiting list for a group session with the queen. Their hive was a-buzz with gossip as swarms of bee-men kept a daily tally. Who scored and who didn't, the losers dashing from the hole in search of the perfect blossom.

I also watched and as had been suggested, I prayed for Casey's safe return. By late afternoon, I was praying for anyone's safe return and hoping my bread would turn out well.

Nightfall came and no Casey. Hungry and scared, I tried sleeping, my head lolling to one side and then the other. I'd awake with every slight sound, a terrible crick in my neck. My pants had been wet some hours before and the coffee cup drained of every last drop.

A slight thump on the outside wall would have brought me to my feet had I not been tied down. It could have been a wild animal foraging for food, or the wind, or any number of harmless possibilities. But it sounded, to me, like a cowboy boot bumping into a log. I waited . . . breathless . . . hoping . . . praying . . .

Minutes passed. I had no idea how many. They seemed like hours. No other sounds, just the faint roar in my ears from too much silence. Then, more thumping sounds behind me.

Someone's out there.

A creak on the other side of the kitchen wall.

The front door.

A cold draft of air raised the hair on the back of my neck.

They've opened it.

Scootching my chair around by pitching my body from side to side, I wobbled it to a spot where I could peer around the doorway.

Can't see. It's too dark.

Wait. Maybe . . . Was that a man's shape? Casey? Oh, please. Let it be Casey. Oh, God. Please let it be Casey.

Heavy boots entered the cabin, clumping across the living room. "Hey, you pretty thing. How'd you like to go for a ride?"

"Casey! It's you. Oh, I'm so glad to see you. Where's the other guys? Oh, come give me a kiss. I'm so glad to see you."

"One of them didn't make it. The one you called Whiskers. The other one's still out there. You OK? Careful. Don't try to stand up too fast. See? Your circulation's been cut off."

"How'd you do it? How on earth did you ever get away from those two?"

"I'll explain later. Right now, we got things to do. I'll get a fire going, and you get some chow ready to eat now and some to take with us."

"Aren't we leaving? Tonight?"

"Yeah. But when we go, we're traveling light. Two days food and a sleeping bag. And that's about it." He stoked the kitchen stove while I made a trip to the outhouse.

By the time I returned, the stove was hot and the kitchen growing warm. I changed into a pair of new jeans from my bag and started to heat some water. Casey had flopped on a kitchen chair. He scratched his head, thoughtfully, then said, "We're going to let him think we're settling in for the night. Then hightail it when nobody's looking."

"You think someone's out there? Waiting for us?"

"Hard telling. That one you call Beard's a little strange. He knows damn well he can't stay here any longer. If I was him, I'd be headed for the Canadian border. But, who knows. I wouldn't put it past him to follow us for awhile. Keeping us in his sights, just for the fun of it. What're you fixing there?"

"Well, there's all this left over rice . . . I can open some more cans. At least it'll be hot and filling."

"That's great for now, but we got to take something with us. Make some biscuits like you did the other night."

"Can't. The biscuit mix's all gone."

"Well, lemme see." He was in the pantry. "Here's flour, baking powder, and . . . Hey! Here ya go. Corn meal. It's just to stir up some cornbread." In two strides, he had reached the table and was busily prying the top off the container.

Red-faced by a wash of guilt, I reached for the corn meal, "Uhm, I can . . ."

"At's all right. I'll do it while you fix the rice. What's this? Keerist Awmighty. Lookee here. It's that floppy disk they wanted. Stuck down here in the cornmeal. Would you believe it?

"Uh, wow! Imagine that."

"You got any tape? Should be a first aid kit here, somewhere." Casey had returned to the pantry and was now selecting boxes at random which he was pawing through until the stuff was either on him, on the floor, or both.

"Second shelf. While you're up there, hand me that can of cayenne pepper." Dumping a spoon or two in the warmed over rice, I examined the can while keeping a sharp eye on his newest stunts. Cayenne pepper was a hellish weapon, when flung into an opponents face. I shrugged, and popped it in my shirt pocket.

Not as good as mace but might come in handy.

Jerking up his shirt, Casey quickly popped the top off the adhesive tape and secured the disk to his bare midriff. "When we get out, I'll need this to prove my case in court."

"What do you mean, `your case in court'? It's these other guys that're the criminals. Not you."

"That's true, except for just one little detail. I had to shoot a guy back there, Kate. With my own gun. He was carrying it on his horse. First chance I got, I took it away from him. There was a fight. I took aim, shot, and left him for dead."

"Ohmigod. Is that what happened to Whiskers?"

"Yep. Might have to do the same thing to at least one more before we get to the ranger station. Is that rice ready? Cornbread can cook while we're eating."

That night, after dishes were washed, we blew out the candles and pretended to go to bed. Casey had fed the horses and rubbed them down. Keeping them inside the barn where they wouldn't be seen, he'd then saddled a fresh mount for himself and one for me. The nice bay we'd found down by the creek. "Just remember," he warned. "If I go down, you're to keep on a-going. Don't stop, don't look around, just get the hell out of these woods. That's a good horse you'll have under you there and if you're not sure which way to go, let him have his head. He's got more mountain sense than either one of us. And he'll go as far as you ask him or until he drops. Whichever comes first."

My throat taut and in serious danger of spouting something soppy, I hugged him as hard as I could and showered kisses on his thin cheeks.

An hour, two hours dragged by. I found it hard to sit for very long, but Casey dozed off almost right away. I waited, pacing barefooted, stretching my leg muscles, and watching him sleep. In the pantry, a mouse rustled in its torn-paper nest and from the wild outside the erratic yapping of a coyote carried on the blowing wind. I was at the window, noting how the tree-tops swayed in the moonlight when he said, "Seems to be as quiet as it's going to get. You ready to go?"

I turned and nodded, ignoring the anxious knot in my gut.

We tip-toed down the path to the barn where Casey propped all of the doors and the corral gates open. We mounted our horses, each of us carrying a container of cornbread tied to the back of the saddle - a sleeping bag, a slicker, and little else. Casey had his gun back, and by the way he carried it, knew full well how to use it. A rifle, slimmer but a little longer than Beards.

"When I give the nod," he said, "slap that horse's butt with the reins as hard as you can and hang on. We're leaving this shack in style."

And that we did. Whooping in loud imitation of a fourth-rate western, we sailed out of the barn, driving the extra horses out the gate and into the woods. I had a hunch, they'd not only be more able to fend for themselves out there but be awfully hard to catch. We then stormed down the path. About a half mile down, Casey veered off the trail and headed into a pine thicket. After a few hours of riding, I recognized the gully where we'd first walked up and saw the deer.

Early morning has always been my favorite part of the day, but I'd never quite known a morning as glorious as this one. It wasn't quite light enough to see much, but the scent of the pines was sharper, the song of the birds heaven-sent. And I didn't even mind the chilly dew that dripped off the leaves and needles making churly knots of my hair. We didn't push the horses, but let them pick their way through the rocks and bushes.

Dawn broke, staining the sky a bright yellow-pink as we neared the compound. The horses were tethered far enough away so that they couldn't be heard and we walked up the trail, hiding behind the same bushes as before. The windows were dark in both the house and the bunkhouse and the almost clear wisps of smoke fading away from the chimneys suggested that since no one had yet stoked the fires, they were all still asleep.

I settled under the same cedar tree and kept the watch. A soft rain began to streak off the cedar boughs and showered the dark green rhododendron bushes, leaving them clean and glistening.

"Stay here," Casey whispered. "I'm gonna check the place out." While he was gone, I finished off the last of my cornbread and thought about our forced walk up here from the lake. A lot had happened since then. That's when I remembered . . . .

The Porsche! I forgot to ask Casey if he'd seen the Porsche when he went back with Black Beard and Whiskers. Funny how fate can completely reorganize a person's priorities. Less than a week ago, I'd have been hell-bent for election to get my car on the road and back to town.

Now, I really wanted to see this case through, to the end. I also remembered my camera. The last time I'd had it was under this very tree . . . I reached up, and there it was. Right where I'd hid it and left it in the rush to get away. Thank goodness for the waterproof case. The camera, my extra film and a notepad was still dry and useable.

About half an hour later, amid a rustle of wet leaves and softly falling footsteps, Casey crawled into my little den. Although the rain had drenched everything in sight, the large, over-hanging branches kept this space dry and cozy. He smiled and showed me his high sign, a firm thumbs-up fist.

"What did you learn?"

"Old Black Beard seems to be part of this group, after all. His horse and saddle's in the barn, took his gear with him. Must have rode directly here after our little skirmish."

"So, you think he's sleeping it off in the bunkhouse?"

Nodding thoughtfully, "Either that or the house," Casey said and parted the cedar branches just enough to see out. Someone was up. A small light gleamed briefly at the window and thick smoke billowed from the rooftop. "Like I say, he didn't put his horse in the corral with the others. It's got its own stall, in the barn."

"He's trying to hide it from you."

"Don't think so. He knows damn well that's the first place I'd look. Besides, a regular hand wouldn't never get away with turning the boss's horse out to put his own in 'ere. And even though that mare of his is a fairly nice three-year old, she ain't no prize. But she was still fed her fill of sweet hay and grain. Naw, that guy's got privileges. And since he's too dumb to be a foreman, I'd say he had connections somehow, to whoever the hell is running this joint."

"Well, like you said. He is a strange one."

For the next ten minutes or so, Casey gazed out from between the branches. He then turned to me and asked, "Mind staying hid a little bit longer? I'd like to check out that warehouse and that big hole out back they been digging."

"I guess not."

"I'll leave the rifle here for you, in case there's any trouble."

"Hey, you better take it. You'll need it more than I will."

"At's all right. You take it anyway. Remember how to use it? If you run into trouble, any trouble at all, it's loaded and ready to shoot." He bent down and laid a wet smack on my forehead. "I'm just gonna sneak out there, look around a little, and sneak back. Won't be gone long."

A gorgeous sunrise of purplish-grey clouds highlighted by a peach-colored sky reminded me how great it was to be alive and free. I snapped a few pictures, using a tall evergreen for depth. But, our situation had not really improved much. A maniacal sharpshooter still kept us from making a run towards home, and I could not stop worrying.

Determined to make myself useful in Casey's absence, I moved around the perimeters of the house and corral taking pictures and making notes. That finished and knowing that the cause of Beard's behavior, and Whiskers too probably, had to have a lot to do with whatever lay buried in that man-made pit, I abandoned my warm nest and took the path towards Casey and the warehouse.

There would have to be an investigation of our charges against the kidnappers, should we live long enough to get them filed. Plus, Casey was sure to feel the heavy hand of law when they heard about the dead Whiskers. Any pictures we could produce of the metal canisters, especially if I could get a close-up of them in the hole, would prove invaluable to our case in court.

With any luck at all, I'd cross trails with Casey before I got there.

12

The trail led over wet, soggy ground and although it was cold and miserable my movements were not going to be heard. A low-lying fog and thick woods muffled almost every sound and sheltered me from the biting wind. The soft clang of a cowbell sounded much farther away than it was, about the length of two city blocks from the house porch. Probably the cook calling the men in to eat breakfast.

Wouldn't mind a tall stack of pancakes myself, right now. A side of ham. Marmalade. Lots of hot coffee. Lord, what am I doing out here in the boonies?

It took about twenty minutes to reach the area of the warehouse. Surrounded by six feet of chain link fence and a roll of barbwire across the top, there was no way I could climb over it without being cut to ribbons. Casey was nowhere in sight.

Now what?

The sun was fully up in a weepy sky, making it a lot easier to see. I walked along the fence, looking for a decent vantage point from which to snap some good shots. The zoom lens should take care of the rest. With any luck, I'd run into Casey somewhere along the way. Hopefully, while everyone else was porking out, thickening their arteries with cholesterol and their thighs with calories, he's had a chance to find something we can use to get off this rock and go home.

In the bottom of a small gully, a sudden flood from the spring rains had unearthed the roots of an old maple tree. Top-heavy, it slumped in the direction of the fence. One large branch thrust across the barbwire, creating a make-shift bridge across the fence from tree trunk to compound grounds. The range of vision from up there would include most of the warehouse, the outside machinery, and a few of the evil-smelling containers. Better than nothing.

As I climbed the tree, small chunks of bark came loose from under my feet and fell onto even larger chunks on the damp ground.

Someone else had already been here and crossed over. Casey. Must have been him. It HAD to have been him. Hopefully, Casey was not dumb enough to let himself get caught. He was probably lurking around the grounds, looking for God-knows-what, but staying out of trouble.

The branch's surface was too narrow and uneven to walk on, with small branches sprouting forth every few inches and the bark was too loose to trust. After several frightening attempts to step around them, I sat down, legs hanging loose on both sides and inched my way around or over each one of the smaller twigs. Again, some of the bark was missing and the twigs broken. More evidence of Casey's having been here.

The roll of barbwire was yet another problem. The branch rested directly on top of it, preventing me from crawling any farther as my feet and pant legs were sure to be entangled in the barbs. And as this branch jutted out away from any others of size, there were no hand-holds should I try to walk across. This meant I couldn't go any farther without falling off. I'd have to settle for whatever shots could be had from here.

With one hand hanging precariously to the twigs and leaves overhead, I cleared a large enough space to take a few pictures. Focusing on a metal drum that seen through the zoom lens seemed to be leaking, it took a minute to realize that a pickup was headed towards the warehouse. The workers were on their way. I swung the camera and made out three faces, wedged into the front seat. And in that minute, from the corner of my eye, I saw Casey creep out of the warehouse and close the door. Too late to run, he jumped behind a canister. The same one I'd been focusing on.

102

The small truck pulled into a graveled area on the far side of the warehouse. Although my field of vision was blocked by the building, from the sounds of a rusty slam and, some minutes later, the roar of a huge diesel engine, the men were gearing up.

The engine roared louder and a huge tractor with half-track wheels like a tank trundled over to the canisters where I'd last seen Casey and scooped up the first two. Hoisting them at a level about 3 feet high, it then veered off toward the pit and disappeared down a gravel incline. There were five left standing. Casey had to be either in or behind one of them.

Darn it Casey, get out of there. A slight movement, no more than a shadow passing from one canister to another, helped me keep track of him. A picture of that guy in the diggings while he has the drums in his possession would save our hides later on with the authorities.

Oh, what the heck. My horoscope before I left home, said something about adventure being good for the soul. I couldn't very well sit safely in a tree and watch that overgrown pot hole become Casey's burial site. Very carefully, I stepped to the end of the branch, over the top of the barbwire. At the very end and inside the fence, I swung down. For the space of a heartbeat, I was suspended a foot or so from the ground. Trying not to think about how I would ever get back out, I let go of the branch. Thudding and then rolling on the ground.

Snapping pictures as I went, a quick sprint brought me to the corner of the warehouse. A small, dirty window afforded a peek inside. I'd taken a gamble and won. The men were all in the pit, mounted on machines of one sort or another.

There was no sign of Casey.

Careful to get a good close-up of the symbol on the cans, a very familiar symbol, I crept on my hands and knees to the edge of the canisters. "Casey," I whispered hoarsely, kicking lightly on the first can. "Are you in there? Casey?" I moved to the other cans, intermittently taking shots of the pit and the men in it. By now, there were two tractors down there with one man on foot hefting a large shovel. "Casey? Quick! Come out while they're not looking."

His answer startled me, coming from inside the building, echoing within its rafters. "Kate? For God's sakes girl, what are you doing? Trying to get yourself killed? Get in here before they see you." He could be right, the first tractor was charging up the hill faster than I ever expected it could move. I darted inside the building just as the driver topped the rise and forged towards two more cans. A last fleeting glance before Casey jerked me behind a partition could have knocked me off my feet.

Beard was driving that tractor!

"Casey. I'm so glad to see you. Did you see who's driving that thing?"

"Yea, I did. That doesn't answer my question. What the hell are you doing here?"

"Taking pictures," I said, proudly showing him I'd found my camera. "These shots of that pit and the men working it, will come in real handy when we get home. Not to mention those smelly cans. Is that stuff what I think it is?"

"Afraid it is, Kath. Nuclear waste. Poison. From over at Tri-Cities."

"That's right! There was a big insert in the Seattle Gazette, last week." A cold dread spilled across my shoulders and down my spine. "Oh, shit, Casey! That stuff is radioactive."

"Better watch it. Don't want to get any of that junk on you. Did you touch anything? Get any on your hands or clothes?"

Shuddering, I tried cleaning my hands on my jeans. "I don't think so. Just the toe of one boot."

"Here's some liquid soap. Quick. Before they get back, squirt a little on that boot and wash your hands real good. There's running water in that basin." Jumping up, he thrust his hands to me, palms up. "Do me, too. Gawd, Katie. Hope you ain't radioactive. Tweak your nose and have you shining at night like a light bulb."

"You know, the Fordham Plutonium-Extraction plant is just the other side of these mountains. We're talking nuclear waste. Tons of it."

"Yep. Five, six hours drive in a truck. Full days ride horseback."

"Well, at least we know what's going on. This compound has been converted to a nuclear waste dumping ground and the people who've given us so much grief are obviously involved in it. I don't know whether to be excited about a big discovery or scared we're gonna die."

"Just wash your hands and face. Scrub them real good. Hurry while them guys are down in the pit. And there's some clean overalls in that cupboard. Take your outer clothes off and put them on. Don't forget the hat."

I hurriedly took Casey's advice, peeling my jeans off and scrubbing over a large basin. The overalls were a one-piece affair, with wide straps going over the shoulders and buttoned with a metal clasp. They were also large enough to stand Casey in one leg and me in the other, with a small shed tucked in to take up the slack.

As I stepped into the denim trousers, the click and grind of the largest tractor grew louder and louder. Obviously, it had dropped into a lower gear and was on its way back. Casey was at the window, watching them. "Ready? They'll be topping that hill any minute. OK, here's the plan. We're gonna walk outta here just like we own the place and mosey over to the pickup. If they spot you, try to act normal. Just one of the guys. Can't afford to be trapped in this building. Don't suppose you remembered to bring that rifle, did you?"

"No. My original intentions were to take some pictures."

He peered around the door, signaling for me to follow his lead. "Here we go. Just do what I do. If we get separated, make your way to the horses and get the hell outta these woods. Don't worry about waiting for me. OK? Ready? Get your hat on. Let's go."

My heart thumping in my throat, we walked, stiff-legged but calm, to the pickup. Just as we piled into the front seat and Casey turned the key to start it, the tractor came into view. Still a good two hundred yards away, they bore upon us, changing into a higher gear while Casey cranked the ignition.

The pickup wouldn't start. "Casey, they've seen us. It looks like Beard's driving. What's wrong with this thing? Hurry. He's coming!"

"Battery's low," Casey said, stomping on the accelerator and pulling knobs. Finally, the engine kicked in with a quickening groan. Casey threw it into reverse, swung the truck out, and headed in a bee-line for the gate.

Behind us, the tractor also swung out in the same direction. They were closer to the gate by a good hundred yards. But they were loosing ground. Although the tractor engine howled as it tore up the road, it could not match the speed of the old Chevy. The race to the gate looked about even.

105

Chapter

13

Fifty feet inside the gate, rifle shots echoed across the hill. The oil gage window in the dashboard exploded, the bullet had to have passed just inches from Casey's hand. More shots, the rearend of the pickup fishtailed, throwing gravel and sliding dangerously close to the ditch.

Rubber slap, slap, slapped the inside fenders. Wheel casings bogged in the soft dirt, spinning uselessly. "Son-of-a-bitch shot out the tires," Casey said, his biceps bulging as he wrestled with the steering wheel.

The tractor was closing in. Only a stone's throw from Casey's side window, the front scoop raised aloft. Rear wheels axle-deep in sandy gravel, the pickup slid into the ditch. Tipped, and started to roll.

"Watch it," Casey shouted, slamming on the brakes. "We're going over." Reaching across my lap to wrench the door handle up, he gave it a hard shove and motioned to the far side of the field. "Jump out and run that way." The pickup was beginning to topple as Casey shoved me along the sloping seat with one boot, scrambling along behind me.

We ran a few yards down the ditch, just far enough to get clear. Casey hustled me along in front of him. He then stopped and gave me a quick peck on the cheek. "Don't look back. Just run," he said, and threw me, bodily, up the bank on the other side.

Less than a full minute later, the tractor bashed into the pickup on the driver's side. The seat buckled, the crumbled door enmeshed into the dashboard.

I glanced back once, making sure Casey was still behind me, vaguely noting that the tractor could not climb the steep bank. I slowed, thinking I'd wait for him to catch up. But again, he shouted at me, gesturing wildly at the woods, "Go, dammit. Just go!"

This time, I did what I was told. I ran. Didn't look back, didn't ask questions, didn't stop to wonder why when Casey seemed to be lagging behind.

Just ran.

After about ten minutes, I could no longer hear his labored breathing behind me at all, only the tractor's screaming clash of gears and roaring groan of the engine.

Never mind. Can't think about that. Can't think about any of it right now.

Lungs heaving, side aching, I ran for all I was worth.

The fence and the old maple tree were dead ahead.

Didn't even slow down.

Cramming one boot toe into the old chain link as far as it would go, I scrambled, squirrel-like, up the side of the fence and grasped the end of the maple branch. Using the same momentum, I pulled myself up, flung one foot over, and swung . . . Amazingly enough, I made it. I looked down, tottering, but hanging tight. The branch wedged in my crotch, was on the wrong side of the rolled barbwire.

The sound of a rifle shot echoed across the valley, then another. On my knees and clutching at leaves, I crawled the length of the branch, dropped to the ground, and tumbled into the creek. It was then, I chanced a peek to look for Casey. He was coming, dragging one foot with a decided limp. He had a hundred yards to go.

Meanwhile, the tractor was gaining at a pretty good clip. Obviously, when he could not scale the steep bank, the driver had been forced to go around to the road. But, in high gear and on a flat stretch, he was bearing down on Casey like a mad bull.

Scoop lowered and going in for the kill.

I felt helpless. Unable to do anything but watch.

He'll be catching up with Casey within minutes.

The man on the tractor didn't seem to have a gun or at least time to use it. The rifle shots were coming from the yard by the warehouse, kicking up sod around Casey's stumbling feet.

This was too much. Casey might be able to make the fence in time, but climbing up or jumping to the branch was out of the question. Back up the tree I went. Peering through the heavy leaf cover, I waited, heart in my throat, hoping, praying he'd have the strength . . . .

He knows he'll never scale the fence without help — and probably thinks I've gone on. I debated a moment, then crawled to the edge of the branch. "Casey! Come on. Run!"

It worked. He seemed to speed up when he saw me. But so did the tractor. I was now in plain view of the driver AND the sniper in the warehouse yard. As expected, after a boom and a grey curl of smoke, a bullet soon snipped a path through the leaves above my head.

With only minutes left, Casey was under me, blowing and heaving in exhaustion. Legs wrapped around limbs and leaves, I stretched as far as I could without falling. "Here. Grab my hand."

Wouldn't reach.

"Jump! Come on, Casey. Grab my hand!"

Still wouldn't reach. Within a hard breath and a heartbeat, the tractor would be on him. Over the sound of its thrashing engine, I screamed, "Go up the fence. He's coming. Jump!"

Finally, our hands clasped. I struggled, holding his weight with one hand, clinging to the branch with the other. I wasn't strong enough, couldn't hold him for too long . . . Using the weight of my body, I leaned across the branch to the other side, gasping with the pain of using my arm as a seesaw. Slowly, my body teetered towards the ground, bringing his up. Once we were on an even keel, Casey was able to hang on with his other hand.

Breaking the hold, we clutched the branch with both hands just as the tractor bashed into the fence directly under our feet. The fence went down, rattling the old tree as it grazed its trunk and shaking it to its very roots.

The old maple should have fallen with the fence, forsaking us to the will of the tractor driver. But that old tree had withstood too many storms. It had seen the rise of that fence and seemed determined to witness its fall. It swayed and cracked and lost some more bark, but that hearty old bastion refused to go down.

The tractor, traveling too fast to stop, trampled the fence like a child's toy and pitched, scoop and all, into the creek bottom.

For the first few seconds, Casey and I simply hung on to the tree and each other. Then dropped, Casey crying out in pain when he hit the ground. His leg had been cut and badly bruised when the pickup rolled but he claimed he could still walk.

The tail of my cotton shirt made a good wrap of his wound even though the bleeding had already stopped. And other than being an emotional wreck, I would also live to see another day and take a few more pictures.

We had not only survived the ordeal but actually had a running chance to escape. It was time to go home. Casey jutted his chin towards the wrecked tractor and said, "Looks like our old buddy is coming around." Indeed, the driver was the one we called `Beard' and as we watched, he was squirming out from behind the steering wheel and pushing on the door of the cab.

"I think it's time we left. Don't you?"

Casey nodded. The pain and the incredible effort of staying alive was beginning to show. It would have been better if he'd have had a chance to recuperate, to wrap his wound and fortify it with a splint. But Beard was on his way out of the cab and probably in better shape than either one of us.

"Let's go," I said to Casey, wishing I could have let him rest a little longer. "I doubt our hairy friend will take kindly to our departure and I don't want to have to fight him."

We headed for the hollow where the horses had been stashed. The path was mostly downhill, and though it wasn't exactly easy walking it was better than uphill. After about a quarter of a mile, Casey broke off a dried limb from a dead tree and used it for a walking stick. Beard wasn't following us yet, but I was sure he would. After he'd gone back for horses, guns, and a small posse. I'd been deliberating on an escape route and it was time I let him in on it. "Casey, Honey. There's something I've got to tell you."

"What's that?"

"I don't think we should go off without that gun you found." Seems to me, especially with your bad leg, it could be quite an equalizer."

"I'd damn sure like to have it about now, but . . ." He shook his head, " I don't think I could make it back up hill and then back again to the horses."

"I know that. But I could. You've got your stick. Why don't you go on with that, it'll take about the same length of time for you anyway whether I'm with you or not, and I can go back to get it. One thing's for certain, they won't be expecting me and they won't know we have a gun."

"I don't like the idea of you going up there, alone. Can't trust that bunch. Not for a minute."

"I know that too. I don't intend to get into a confrontation of any kind, I'm just going to grab your gun and get out. Quick as I can."

"But . . ."

"No buts, Casey. They've got horses and guns, too. Sharpshooters, even. Remember? How far would we get? With the horses AND your rifle, we just might be able to even the score enough to get the hell out of here." I hugged him, knowing his ego had taken even more of a beating than his poor leg.

"Guess I ain't used to having a woman play nursemaid for me," he admitted. "Always before, I took care of my own problems."

"I know. And as soon as we're back to a more civilized jungle of mere muggings and petty street crimes, you will again. Promise." Playfully, I crossed myself. "Scouts honor. Now give me a kiss and go get the horses ready. I'll be right there."

He looked terribly forlorn and abandoned, stumbling through the pines on his handmade cane and I felt so sorry for him I almost turned back. But these guys were not the least bit bashful about blowing holes in anyone who had different ideas than theirs and I truly believed we were still not, pardon my pun, out of the woods yet.

I took a more or less direct route, going around the steepest parts but keeping a map of sorts in my head as to where I was and what direction the house would be. There didn't seem to be any sort of a path going in the right direction, but the dense undergrowth that made hiking so tough around the other trees didn't seem to grow too well in a pine forest.

It was well into mid-day by the time I was back in my hiding spot under the big cedar. I was so hungry, I felt faint but still able to unearth my stash of plastic-wrapped jerky and cheese strips. With shaking hands, I ate half of them and saved the other half for Casey.

111

An open window faced this way, and I could hear the sound of loud talking. From the amount of bustle and activity, I had to guess that Beard had been brought to the house, bruised and irate. Quickly, I replaced the spent roll of film in my camera, letting it hang loose from the leather case, and grabbed Casey's rifle. Everything else went into the little knapsack I'd brought from the line cabin. With a last look-around, I made ready to leave my hideout for the last time.

Suddenly, a woman and two men stormed out of the house and headed for the barn. The men I recognized as the truck drivers we had first encountered on the road. There was something engaging about the woman as she was dressed in a forest ranger outfit and had the big, black sheep dog on a leash. They were headed for the barn.

Beard was not among them.

The only one to hear the buzz and click of my camera as I took some fairly decent head shots in profile, was the dog. He immediately lunged in my direction, pulling against his leash, barking ferociously. "Shut up, Lucky," she cried, jerking him back to her side and boxing his ears. "Knock it off."

One of the truck drivers peered into the bushes in the same direction the dog had lunged. "Let him go," he said. "Could be, he picked up her scent already."

"Let him go, hell. And let them know we're on the trail?"

The raised voices and angry gestures only served to excite the dog and make him even more eager to grasp my throat in his bared teeth. Again, he lunged at me, pulling the woman along several steps. She only had one hand to hold him with, her other hand grasped a pouch of the kind I'd seen hanging from the sides of motorcycles.

Again, the dog lunged, breaking her grasp on the leash. In six or seven bounds, he had invaded my hidyhole. But to my surprise, he didn't want me. He had plunged, nose-first, front feet clawing at the earth, into the hole where the plastic wrappers from my dried beef sticks had been buried. As quietly as I could, while the dog gouged at the tree roots and the angry mob cursed and complained, I was making tracks. Whipping past the bushes, running to the spot where I'd agreed to meet Casey and the horses.

It took them a good ten minutes to reroute the dogs efforts and sic him on my trail. I judged myself to be almost half-way to the horses. Once on track, the dog bounded down the trail after me.

As he came alongside, barking and nipping at my ankles, I broke open one of the beef jerky packets. In as friendly and fun-filled voice as I could muster, I said, "Here boy. Have a goody." I kept running. "Mmmm. Isn't that good? Want another?" After the second beef stick and three cheese strips, the dogs chase became more of a romp. Tongue lolling back, ears flapping, he yipped, and when the narrow path would permit, he bounded around me in circles, catching bits of cheese and beef in his wide jaws.

By now, I was getting quite winded and seriously considering a rest, when shouts from behind stirred me on to a faster pace. "Lucky. Here, Lucky. Come on, boy." The dog's ears pricked up at the mention of his name but made no show of turning back. Instead, with a bright-eyed woof, he happily plucked another bite of beef from mid-air and bounded down the path ahead of me.

Oh, well. By the size of those paunch bellies, they're in worse shape than I am. If I can't keep ahead of this crew, I deserve to be caught.

I didn't plan on a tumble. It just happened. It also stunned me for a moment, leaving me sprawled on the forest floor. I awoke to the huff of the dog's beef-peppered breath in my face and the lick of his sloppy tongue. Just then, his ears pricked up and he gazed, guiltily, down the path from where we'd come.

The mob had arrived. "Lucky, dammit. When you gonna learn to come when you're called?"

The one called Ralph ran up to me. "Hey, Joe. Lookie here. I found her."

Still on the ground, the thrum of horses' hooves vibrated under my hands just seconds before Casey burst into view. There was just time to roll off the path under a rhodie bush as he drove his horse into this pack of illiterate nincompoops. Amid many curses and shouts, he led the second horse up alongside me and shouted, "Get on. Hurry!"

I wasn't quick enough and there was no way I could mount a moving horse. The Ranger Woman was a better horseman, which wasn't saying much, and she grabbed the horses bridle just under his chin. "Oh, no you don't. You're not going anywhere."

Casey's horse plunged off the trail then back again as he fought the strong animal, trying to turn it around. I finally remembered the rifle clutched in my left hand. Thought about trying for Ranger woman's groin but knew I'd never be able to actually shoot anyone. Instead, I pointed it at the heavens and pulled the trigger. Boom! The sound alone was enough to scare the bejeesus out of the mob and me too. It severely bruised my shoulder.

Most of all, it terrified the horses. Rearing up, hooves held aloft with whinnying shrieks, they fought their bits and tried to bolt. Casey managed to stay somewhat affixed to the horse's back by clutching the saddle horn with one hand and the reins of my horse with the other. By now, the bay I was to ride was thoroughly panic-stricken. Flinging drool and sweat in a frenzy of bucking and rearing, he bashed into anyone or thing which would attempt to hold him prisoner, including the woman. He gave a great, if too close, interpretation of a rodeo bronc.

In order to keep from being conked by the thrashing hooves, the two men shrank into the woods and ducked behind a tree. Ranger Woman also lost her hold on his bridle and my trusty steed thundered down the path in the direction of the house.

Casey's horse wheeled, grasped his bit with a snot-flinging snort, and followed him.

Chapter

 14

Obviously, I was not yet to ride out of here. I would have cursed my sorry state and the damn fools who had made it so, if I'd had the time and the necessary breath to speak. Instead, I used the few precious minutes I had before the others regained their questionable status as thinking human beings, to reconsider my situation.

I could always run for the shelter of the thick forest. And get myself lost in the process, with no food or shelter, wandering the hills like a hermit gone mad. Or, I could run after Casey and the horses, which would place me back under the gun of Beard and his sharpshooter.

It was a tough decision to make. But, my best bet was to retrieve my mount, hopefully Casey would soon have him under control, and together, he and I could stay ahead of this bunch. With very little energy left, I began a slow jog after Casey.

Ranger Woman was the first to give chase. Her huge, bull-like bosom would have served her well in a strangle hold, but only weighed her down when it came to keeping up with my running jog. The chase lasted little more than five minutes, she losing ground almost from the start. Obviously sour from the taste of biting my dust, she called to her squad like a drill sergeant, "Catch her, you damn idiots. Let her get away this time, and I'll personally cut off your balls and feed them to the pigs."

Not surprisingly, the men began a spirited chase after me, closing the gap after only ten or fifteen yards.

By now, I'd gone past exhaustion ... blundering along on nerve alone. Head swimming, blind to all but the bleary spot of earth where my next foot would fall, I stubbornly stayed erect and moving.

A corner of my mind sensed more than saw a movement, comprehension took a little longer. A brown, hairy forequarter lunged past me, then pulled up. Pummeling the soft earth with its sharp hooves. Through the lung-wrenching pain in my side and the awful sound of my own wheezing, Casey's voice floated past as if borne along on a breeze.

I heard my name. "Kathy?"

With consciousness fading and a sense of the ground coming up to smack me, I tried a half-hearted grin and said, "Hey, guy. Where ya been?" Suddenly, I felt my fingers being pried loose, realized I'd been clutching Casey's gun. Strong arms lifted me up, legs flying askew, and I was plopped unceremoniously upon my old pal, the brown bay. The warmth of the slick saddle and his breadth between my thighs roused me enough to take the saddle horn in my own two hands.

"Come on, Kath. Stay with me, here. Can you ride?"

"Yea. I can ride."

"You sure? I'll lead the horse. You just hang on."

"I'm all right."

"Ok. Let's go then."

The boom of a rifle startled the horses but this time Casey had a firm grip on them both and they didn't bolt.

"You ready?"

I ducked my head in a weak nod.

Another boom and Casey's horse thundered down the trail, his muscular haunches bunched as he gathered speed.

My horse leaped in response to Casey's steel grip on his reins. He seemed glad to be given direction. Trees flew past us in a greenish-brown blur as the bay settled into an easy lope. Somehow, I managed to stay on.

It couldn't have been ten minutes before the house loomed into view. It seemed like hours. Suddenly, the cedar tree and my hidyhole whizzed by in one galloping stretch. Next came the storage shed, the yard . . .

Any minute now, the horses would skid to a standstill . . .

Why doesn't he stop? But Casey didn't even slow down. His heels dug into his horses flank, urging him on, closer and closer to the house. Both horses' momentum increased.

Directly in front of the porch, I felt the bay pause . . . fought, momentarily, the dig of my heels into his side . . . then, still following Casey's lead, he jumped. Both horses landed on the broad front porch, their iron-shod hooves skidding on the old wooden planks.

With a tooth-jarring thud, the bay bashed into the front door. The force of his moving weight and mine, tore the hinges from the aged wooden frame. And with a screaking rip, it gave way, creating a jagged, gaping hole.

Inside the house, a long hall stretched out before us. Daylight played on the floor for the first four or five feet, the rest lay hidden in shadow.

The horses snorted and pranced nervously on the wooden plank porch. Casey swung down from his mount, slapped its rear, and sent it leaping to the front yard. Still holding the reins to my horse, he held out his other arm to help me slide off.

The heavy front door was mostly still solid, even though the hinges had been ripped loose and hung from the frame in splinters. We ducked in, taking care not to get scratched. Halfway down the hall and to the left was a staircase going up. What looked like built-in cupboards closed off the space under the stairwell.

A small room, off to the right, looked like a kitchen. I followed Casey in, immediately crouching in the corner between the inside wall and a wood cook stove. Listening intently, Casey gestured with a finger to his lips that we should stay quiet. I tried, but couldn't stop wheezing.

He relieved me of my small backpack, pawing through the contents to find the shells to his rifle. Loaded and cocked, we listened intently for a warning sound, any sound, from the other inhabitants. So far, they had all been accounted for except for the one I'd bashed over the head outside the storage shed, and Beard. There could very well be more.

When my breathing had returned to normal, Casey indicated that he was going into the next room and that I should stay put. No dice.

Each time we'd separated in the last few days, we'd taken turns battling these hoodlums on our own. I noiselessly but emphatically shook my head and got up. We'd gotten in this mess together, and live or die, we'd see it through. Together.

The kitchen was the front end of a large L-shaped room. Since we could see the back end of a chair and table, the other end was probably a dining/family room. Any one of them could be holed up in there. They certainly knew the house and where to find its many possible hiding places.

Rifle poised and cocked, Casey darted a quick peek around the corner. When he seemed satisfied, he gestured to be quiet and follow him. We went in, carefully tiptoeing around the inside corner. The room, though fairly long, held little else besides a large, sturdy table, eight chairs, and a crudely-built hutch.

Quietly, we made our way to the far end which opened up to a larger room. A line of shelves on the inside wall faced a stone fireplace in which the remains of a large log smoldered and snapped. Cotton drapes covered a bay window, shutting out the world and preventing anyone else from looking in. From there, a front door led to what I presumed was a yard.

An old piano reposed in one corner.

When Casey had satisfied himself by peering behind each couch and chair, we went back to the kitchen. The door to the hall was still open. A shudder ran through me at the sight of the dark hall. Had Beard come down from upstairs? Were there more men we hadn't yet seen? I didn't want to find out the hard way. I made a tiny sound in my throat, hoping to stop Casey's progress as he crept across the kitchen. He paused, obviously waiting for me to explain.

I was expected to be specific.

He already knew it was dangerous. And he already knew I was scared. *How do I explain that the creepy tingle across my scalp and the bellyful of dread seemed to be focused on that shadowed stairwell?*. Again, I shook my head at him and grimaced. He quickly faded into the corner with me, waiting breathlessly to see if anyone would show their face.

In less than a count of five, a familiar, bearded head appeared, gazing intently away from us, in the direction of the dining room. He'd kept track of our movements enough to know we'd gone in there, but had not noticed we'd come back.

As his head poked through the doorway, the rifle in Casey's hands swung, thwacking Beard dead center in the back of his neck. He staggered, blinked at me in surprise, then slumped to the floor. "Get something to tie his hands," Casey hissed, and instantly leaped into the dark hall. Poised, and, if necessary, ready to shoot. But evidently, Beard was working alone. After a careful search, Casey came back to the kitchen.

Although he'd stumbled and seemed confused, Beard had never totally lost consciousness. Face to the floor, his eyes followed my every move. He didn't try to speak, didn't resist my efforts to bind his hands with an old dishtowel.

The minute I finished, Casey tugged on the knot, making sure it would hold. "It's a little loose. Look around for some tape. Might be some in those cupboards."

On each side of the front door jamb was a prop, built long ago to hold each end of a 2X4. In place, it would prevent all but a heavy tractor from bashing the door down. Thank goodness, it hadn't been up when we hit it with our horses. We'd probably still be outside, nursing their wounded shoulders.

After Casey took quick stock of the back yard from the porch, he shoved the door back in place and set the board into the props. He'd found a hammer and nails in the pantry and proceeded to pound the hinges back onto the door frame. With everything nailed shut, we had a fairly solid barricade. He then waggled a thumb in that direction. "Watch for that screwy bunch outside to show up. I'm gonna check upstairs."

The drawers next to the sink held little more than some mismatched silverware. An old shoebox in the small pantry bulged with odds and ends and a few more tools but no tape. I did find a roll of thick, pliable wire. This I used on Beard. By twisting it around his wrists on top of the rag, it would keep him tied up without cutting off the circulation. I then sat down to wait.

Beard continued to watch me.

An alarming thump from upstairs and what sounded like a child's cry, startled me out of a weary lull. I'd sank back down into the corner between the wood stove and the wall to rest, and almost went to sleep. The thought that I could actually doze off in the midst of this much conflict only went to convince me just how tired I really was.

A few minutes later, two sets of boots tramped down the stairs, and again, I heard that same strange wail and snivel. It was definitely too deep-throated to be a child, too unrestrained to be a man. A quick glance at Beard's face revealed little, other than the fact that he was riled.

Casey hustled in another little guy whose age it was impossible to tell. He was overweight, balding, wringing his small, soft hands, and crying. A fresh bandage stretched across the bridge of his nose. "I didn't do nothing. It's not my fault."

He seemed to bear a resemblance to Beard, although it showed up in an odd way. Where Beard had dark, almost porcupine-stiff hair, this man's hair was soft, thin, and cut short around the temples. Beard's complexion, what we could see of it, was ruddy and tough as leather. The other's was pinkish, with round soft cheeks and lacking in facial hair. Fleshy jowls wobbled when he chattered, in place of a heavy beard.

Still, I couldn't quite get over the idea that there was a resemblance. When he spoke to Beard, I was even more convinced. "Tell them, Bubba. I didn't do nothing. It not my fault."

"Shut up. Nobody's sayin' you did. Just sit down and shut up. And you won't get hurt."

On Beard's command, the little guy's jaws clamped together. He stumbled to a chair, clearly terrified, more than, I believed, of Beard than us. He plucked the bandage nervously.

There was something familiar about the child-like scramble, something niggling at the corner of my mind. *I'd think of it later.* For now, I gently patted his arm. "We're not here to hurt you." When he relaxed, I turned to Beard, and said, "In fact, we've been trying to get out of these mountains for a week now, but we have to keep dodging bullets."

The little guy's attention wavered as I spoke, seeming to settle on the last word he'd heard and comprehended. "Bubba's got bullets. I seen 'em. And he said I could have some, too." He began to pull at his jacket pockets, tearing at the white cotton in his excitement. "See? I told you. Bubba said I could keep 'em." There, in his moist, soft palm lay a handful of empty shells.

Suddenly, Casey snatched the shells from his hands. "Where'd you get these?"

The little guy reacted as before, kicking his feet and clenching his pink little hands in anxiety. "Give me back my bullets.

Those are mine. Bubba? He stole my bullets. You said I could keep them."

Had I been able to, I would have walked out on these machomales and sworn the rest of my life to celibacy. The little guy's childlike ways could not be helped and were quite understandable. The others were not. "Casey, for crying out loud. Give those back to him." By now, the little guy was almost hysterical, banging his head into the back of his chair in a frantic rocking motion.

"I'm not taking his damn bullets. I just wanted to know where he got them. These are 20/40s. Which are damn few and far between. They fit this carbine, here," he said, and hefted the rifle he'd been carrying. To me, he said, "I trust you'll remember just where this rifle came from."

So much had happened in the last ten days, I'd almost forgotten our first brush with death. The body of the cowboy, the lifeless lake, and, later on, a horse and mule found tangled in the brush with a load of supplies and this particular rifle. It had been in our possession, ever since. Those bullets had to have been fired before we ever left Seattle and possibly by the cowboy himself.

I nodded my head, and said, "I remember. But you don't need all of them, do you? There must be half a dozen of them there. Let him keep all but two." Scooping them out of Casey's open hand, I handed them to the little guy.

Evidently, my act of kindness jarred the little guys memory. He remembered something all right. He remembered me. Stuffing the shells back in his pocket, he turned his frightened, innocent face to me, he said, "Sister says I'm not supposed to stay in the shed. I tried to do what you said, but she told me to come in the house." He shivered. "It's too cold for me to be out."

Ohmigod. No wonder he seemed familiar. This was the guy I'd clobbered in front of the shack. He'd had a bloody nose and a seizure, making him a little hard to recognize. But that was no excuse. Awash with guilt, I stumbled back into my corner. "I'm so sorry. I . . . I didn't know. I never should have hit you."

"It's OK, Missus. Maybe we could be friends? I got lots more things I saved. You want to come to my room and see? I got a special . . ."

Beard grouched from the floor. "Hate to break up this little love fest, but have you considered what you're going to do about the guys outside? If you think they're gonna just go away, you better think again."

"You know," said Casey. "I hate to agree with him, but we'd best find a better place to hide than this room."

"Untie me, and I can help," Beard said.

"Why would you want to help us?"

He shrugged, looking at Casey, the little guy whom I had decided was probably his brother, and me. "Why not? There ain't no more future in this. I told them they'd get caught sooner or later. I was about to hightail it anyway, just didn't know what to do about Jimmy."

"I'll untie your feet so you can go upstairs with us. But you're going to have to do more than that before we can trust you."

Of the three bedrooms upstairs, one had twin beds. Jimmy ran in and carefully saved his shells in a small metal box. I worried about him being left to race through the house. God only knew what that mob had told him about us and how he might react. In his childlike innocence, he could put all of us in danger. But since I'd rather endure all of hell's fury than tie the little guy's hands again, I'd just have to deal with it.

The second bedroom surprised me. Perched upon the pillow of a frilly bedspread was a stuffed animal, a white bear in a dress and matching hat, standing guard over one lonely atomizer of perfume and a worn lipstick. Somehow, surrounded this past ten days by bullies and machomales, I would have expected Ole' Ranger Woman to favor something more along the line of leg irons, leather whips and chains.

But the third room was the most interesting. It had an outdated computer, hooked up to a couple of old car batteries, a metal filing cabinet, and dozens of dusty boxes stacked four high and marked with the date and a number of abbreviations which undoubtedly meant something to somebody. From what I could see, the dates went back some twenty years.

The computer was an ancient one, built long before the days of microchips, and about the size of a small refrigerator. The floppy disk Casey now carried would fit just fine.

After watching him pull tape and belly hair, I said to Casey, "You go downstairs and make sure that mob doesn't get in. Let them be out in the cold for awhile. Beard . . . you know, if you'd tell me your name it would help."

"The name's Jack. Jack and Jimmy Gillespie."

"OK, Jack. If you'll sit down and answer all my questions and even offer some informative comments, I promise not to have Casey bash you over the head."

Jack, in my head I still thought of him as Beard, seemed to be ready to cooperate. Which meant, he would talk. Evidently, he now saw Casey and I as the dominant ones. We had the house, we had guns, and we had him tied up. Obviously, we were in power. Plus, I had a hunch he was nursing a bit of a crush on Yours Truly.

As I switched the computer on and waited for it to warm up, I said, "Where in the world do we start? What are you people doing up here and what is the deal with that pit? Tell me all you know about those containers and where they came from."

Beard looked at me, and if his face hadn't been covered with so much hair, I would have sworn he blushed. "Janice," he said. "I guess you know by now that she's a forest ranger and our sister to boot, caught some asshole trying to dump a truck load of hazardous waste up here in the woods. Some of that nuclear waste from the plant over in Eastern Washington. Told him he'd have to pay, or she'd turn his ass in to the authorities. He could afford it. Made out damn good, money wise. Got paid for transporting the stuff all the way to some desert location out in Utah, which he never did do, of course. Kept the dumping fee, too. A nice little bit of change, I wanna tell ya. And alls he had to do for all that money was haul it up the road aways, coming this way from the east side of the Cascades, and store it till he or one of the crew could bury it out there in the pit. Forged all the documents and passed around a little payola. No problem. To make a long story short, him and my sister got all cozy. Even shacked up for awhile, here in the house. That's when I left and took up residence in the line shack up on Green Mountain. Same place where we took you and that bean pole of a boyfriend of yours. Anyway, where was I?"

"You were making a long story short."

"Oh. Yea. Well, this cowboy'd been working for some outfit for some time. Hauling nuclear waste way down to Oregon and all kinds of places. We all decided, that money could go a long ways in making up what we was due. And why shouldn't we? That fuckin' place ruined us. We all grew up downwind from the plant, over by the Tri-cities and never knew about that damn plutonium leakin' and blowin' till it was too late. I mean, what the run-off did to the land and the crops. Took our farm, by making it so damn polluted it wouldn't grow nothing no more. Calves and sheep all born dead or deformed. Killed our parents, God bless 'em. Worked their hearts out all their lives trying to make a go of a farm, and raise a bunch of kids to be God-fearing Christians and know the difference between what's right and what's wrong. And what the government's doing over there is dead wrong. Our parents went on to an early grave, because of it. I'm tellin' you, the Bible says, 'An eye for an eye.' Oh, the doctors all said that they died of natural causes. And that's the biggest bunch of bullshit I ever heard. Since when is it natural for two people, who never drank a drop of liquor their whole lives or smoked a single cigarette, to both get cancer on their insides. Liver, kidneys, everything went all at once. Eaten up by it. They died within two years of each other. Natural deaths my ass. That fuckin' place poisoned us, took our parents in what shoulda been the prime of their lives, leaving us to fend for ourselves when I was barely in my teens. Toxins everwhere. The water, the air, even the damn earth that grew this nation's food supply. Crammed with it. And here's our Mamma breathing in them gaseous fumes all the time she was carrying us, and eating and drinking that poison day after day. Made my twin brother a nitwit. You're damn right we're gonna get what we can, and then some. Fuckin' Fordham owes us."

Head reeling from Jack's account of his family history and his odd habit of mixing four letter words with Scripture, I noticed the computer had finally finished warming up. As privately as possible and feeling Jack's eager black eyes boring into my back, I inserted the floppy disk and proceeded to take the steps which would hopefully bring it up on the screen. With any luck at all, this disk would contain some hard evidence to either disclaim or back up Jack's allegations.

I logged on, only to find a password-protected menu which refused to unlock. "Jack, this old system isn't exactly user friendly. All I'm getting is a series of blinking numbers and letters. There has to be some sort of a code."

His only answer was a noncommittal shrug.

"Well, surely you at least know the password. Or where I can find it. I've got to have it in order to get in."

124

"Shoot, don't ask me. I don't know how to work the damn thing. It's all a bunch of mumbo-jumbo anyway, you wanna know the truth. Computers, robots, machines . . . whatever happened to the idee that should a man want to pass something on to another, he could damn well write it down."

I had to laugh, pleased that Jack had decided to help. In fact, once he opened the gates and started talking, the flood of foul language and epithets was hard to close. It could mean that his loyalties were for sale to the highest bidder. But I doubted it. The ultimate price had already been paid with the demise of the family farm and lives of their parents. And I had a sneaking hunch that Jack was smarter than he looked.

"It would make things easier," I said, with an affirmative nod. "But for now, this program has me locked out until I can determine the password. What year were you and your brother born?"

"1962." Jack's mouth twisted in his thick beard. "That's the same year all the lambs belonging to the other farmers, was born deformed and our prize calf, a purebred Angus bull with a bloodline as long as my arm and that includes four blue ribbons, was born dead. Daddy paid a purty penny for that insemination. Lost it all. March 12, 1962 is our birthday."

Almost overwhelmed with the series of events Jack's family had experienced, it was hard to concentrate on an old computer program. But, I had to. The information on this disk could very well have been the motive for at least one man's death and possibly the reason why Casey and I had been put through such torment. This may be the only way of gaining access to it.

Taking a deep breath and forcing my mind to stay on the task at hand, I continued to ask pointed questions. "Do you remember your sister's year of birth and date?"

"1958. July, I think. Yea. July 27th."

"Ok. How about your parents?"

"Hell, I don't know."

"All right, what day did they die?"

"Uh, I remember it happening like it was yesterday, but, I couldn't say what actual day it was."

I tried what dates I had on the program, using them as number combinations and letters. Swapping them around, backwards, forwards, doubling them, tripling them. Nothing worked. The program continued to blink numbers and a few letters.

Jack was whispering, I suddenly realized it wasn't to me. "What you doing in here?"

Jimmy was in the other chair, playing with a yo-yo. Quietly he began to recite, off tune, the words to his favorite song. "Jesus loves me, this I know. For the Bible . . ."

Jack colored, seemingly embarrassed. "Jimmy, take your yo-yo in the bedroom. Go on. I'll be there in just a little while." To me, he said, almost apologetically, "He's a little out of kilter. Any kind of break with his regular way of doing things gets him all confused. He's got to have familiar stuff around him. And a set schedule. He don't mean to bother nobody."

"No bother at all," I replied, smiling at Jimmy as reassuringly as possible. Indeed, Jimmy's presence at this time was not the problem. But what would he do if a real fight broke out? If we all ran for our lives? Would the bunch we'd been referring to as the mob take his state of mind into consideration before they fired on us? Or would they save their own necks and worry about Jimmy later on?

Returning my attention to the computer screen, I asked Jack, "What have we forgotten? There have to be some other dates we're not using." Jack honestly tried, but he couldn't remember, offhand, his parents birthdays, or the dates they died. I was about ready to throw in the towel when I realized that Jimmy's singsong had changed. It was now in months and numbers. When I listened even closer, I realized it was in dates. "November 15, Fifty eight, August 1, forty two, September 23, sixty three, January 4, sixty four, April 18, sixty eight."

Was it possible . . . "Jimmy. This is important. Are those the numbers for the password on this program?"

"November 15, fifty eight, . . .

Puffing his chest out with pride, Jack indicated his brother and said, "Isn't he something'? It's a kind of genius with him. We're sort of opposites. I couldn't remember my own shoe size if my life depended on it. But Jimmy here, never forgets a number or any kind of number combinations. Alls he has to do, is hear it once and he's got it. Committed to eternal memory."

"Numbers?" It dawned on me that Jimmy, in his own sweet, little way was trying to help. I hurriedly typed; the numbers and the first letter of each month, as he sang. When he stopped singing, I paused . . . waited to see if he'd continue and to see if the computer would spit them out with a cranky squeak. After a moment, I hit enter. Accompanied by a lot of clicking and grinding sounds, the menu magically opened.

It was all text. No mouse, no cursor, just informative text as if it were an assortment of reports and letters. Mostly by a Dr. Robb. No wordprocessing functions, one just scrolled up or down.

According to the report, samples of earth gathered from the area, with varying levels of toxicity and radioactive contamination, had been tested. This was prefaced by a theory of what might happen should these emissions be allowed to continue. Page after page, Dr. Robb elaborated as to the dangers of the testing of nuclear waste materials and the general production of plutonium. These were documented and backed up by their findings in the community, as to their effect on nonhuman life.

Them came the studies of humankind. It rankled me when this doctor seemed hesitant to call these mortals by their real names. The closest he came was a Jane and John Doe, living within X number of miles of the reactors, who suffered terribly. All this was in medical terms, but seemed to be referring to the poor health of numerous patients in nearby hospitals. I recognized, by name, several types of cancer and a kind of thyroid disease. Other reports listed evidence derived from studies done on volunteers from several schools in Washington state and Oregon. It was all interesting and terribly close to home, but not exactly something worth a man's life. Anyone could have found the same facts in a good, public library.

By now, Casey was back in the room, peering over my shoulder. I continued to scroll the computer screen down, hoping that I'd find something, anything that would make all of what we'd been through, worthwhile.

Suddenly, the screen opened up to an itemized report labeled top-secret with all the warnings and trappings of a national security risk. "Bingo." Jack and Casey looked to me for a better explanation, while Jimmy seemed content enough to play with his yo-yo.

"This is data on secret experiments, aimed at determining the effects of radiation on human reproductive organs. You know, there's a lot of medical terms and governmental hocus pocus, but according to the above report, the levels of radioactive materials they used were pretty high. Hmmm. They all seem to have been done or at least supervised by this same Doctor Robb. Some kind of scientist, not on the staff. Evidently, Fordham contracted out some of their projects. I wonder where he is now."

The reports were fascinating, and at times, overwhelming. "Wait. Here's a test showing what levels of radioactive pluto-nium will produce certain reactions . . . Oh. Here we go. Ohmigod. Good grief! Look at this. They radiated these men in their . . . How in the world . . .!"

Did these guys know at the time, what the tests were all about? What man would knowingly consent to having his testicles shot with a carcinogen? I continued reading quietly, deciphering what I could from the terminology.

Jimmy had gone back to his favorite pastime: reciting the words to old gospel songs, in his odd, three-note chant. Some of them were familiar, even though I was sure the original score had more of a melody. Normally, I would have preferred to study the infor-mation on the disk when I was alone and more able to concen-trate. But Jimmy was mostly quiet, agreeable, and I found I en-joyed his company. It struck me that his memory banks provided the only access I had to this program. "Jimmy, do you remember those numbers? The dates? Can you tell me what they are again?"

His reaction to being pressed for information caught me a little off guard. Suddenly, his blank, innocent stare took flight -- bouncing from the walls to the window like a bird entrapped in the room. He began to hyperventilate.

Gently, I patted his trembling hands. "It's OK, Jimmy. Calm down, now. We can do this some other time. I didn't mean to frighten you." Awash with guilt for causing Jimmy's distress, I said to Jack, "The data on this disk may be the only substantial proof we have, not only for us but your family, too. It could very well save our hides and explain what happened to your parents. The problem is, this computer is such an old, clunky thing, I'm afraid to keep it on the screen for more than an hour or so at a time. Who knows how long these car batteries will hold? I'll have to close it down pretty soon. But without access to it later on, I . . ."

Jack nodded, showing me he understood, then gave Jimmy a brotherly poke in the ribs. "Hey, cool it. The lady's just asking some questions. That's all."

After a few minutes, obviously trying to find a rote that he could be comfortable with, Jimmy returned to his favorite sing-song. "Jesus loves me, this I know. For the Bible tells me so. Little ones . . ."

Scared that any future access to this program may be forever forgotten, I waited until he finished his song, then nudged him as gently as I could onto another track, beginning with a few dates. "November 15, 58, December 23, 59 . . ."

Jimmy jerked as if he'd been jolted by an electronic impulse, then acted as if he'd been insulted. Evidently, my dates were wrong and I'd misquoted him. Highly offended, he began to correct me. This time, I was ready with pencil and paper in hand, and jotted them down. "November 15, 58, AUGUST 1, 52," he said, his soft lips turned down at the corners in a pout. If anything, Jimmy knew what he knew and had no patience for some numskull such as myself who could not recall on demand, a simple group of dates. Albeit they were some forty numbers long.

"OK," I said, powering down the computer and slipping the disk into my coat pocket. "We better take care of the present. House all locked up? Have any idea what happened to the others?"

Casey nodded. "I boarded everything up as well as I could. Unless they come in a second floor window, I don't see how they'll ever get in. Won't be from the front door, that's for damn sure." At the lower landing, he pointed out the boards he'd nailed over the door frame. "As far as that's concerned, we'll have an even tougher time getting out."

As we tromped down the stairs, I was struck by the opposites manifested by the twins. Jimmy skipped from step to step, humming happily, lost in a world only he could understand but in which he seemed much more gratified than we were in our own. Directly behind him, Jack's boots thumped belligerently, his beard casting a black shadow over his face and neck as he darted hateful glances at Casey.

My stomach was growling with hunger. "I suppose we'd all better have a bite to eat. If you want to build a fire in the kitchen stove, I'll try to round up something for supper. No promises, but there might be something down there I can fix. Don't count on any bread."

Outside, the wind had come up and the sun had gone down. A woman and two men had been locked out of their own home and we had locked ourselves in. Who were the bad guys, now?

Oh, well. As they say in the suburbs . . . life must go on.

Chapter 15

Late that night, I awoke to the sounds of an old house being battered by the wind and Casey's snoring. It was a wonder I had slept at all. In between his puffing and nasal gasps, boards creaked in the walls, sending ghoulish visions through my sleep-deprived mind. Outside, a full moon displayed the evergreens in stark silhouette and the bony joints of a tree limb scratched the windows.

Casey and I had sprawled, fully dressed and exhausted, across the bed in the sister's room amid a menagerie of stuffed animals. Sleeping in someone else's bed, even under normal circumstances was tough. This was proving to be impossible. I tried turning Casey on his side, several times. It didn't help. He snored even louder and began to mutter.

Leaving him to rattle the rafters alone, I crept out of bed and foraged along the dresser top for a match and candle. That found, and sheltering the puny flame with my palm, I slipped down the hall and closed myself back in the office.

That afternoon, I'd noticed a stack of old boxes, crammed with papers that had yellowed with age along the edges. They were piled head-high along one entire wall and part of another. At the time, I'd thought they'd probably held a lot of boring book-keeping notes and saved receipts. But, boring was better than the cacophony of sound emanating from the bedroom and the snooping at least kept my over-alert mind off more middle-of-the-night appraisals of our situation.

Blowing the dust off the top box, I placed it in the center of the floor. If the dates on the outside flap were any indication of how old they were, Fordham's recorded history from some thirty years ago had been stored, if not hidden, here.

Picking one of the boxes at random, I carefully removed some crumbly tape. Inside, an official-looking stamp on every page warned me in faded red ink that this was TOP SECRET stuff. Evidently, only those with the right security clearances from the upper echelons of Fordham dared decipher one single word. Of course, for me, it only served to heighten my curiosity.

I delved into the depths of the box and began a search of its contents. Having no idea of where to start, I plucked out a few papers and sat down to read.

A rambunctious flock of birds gave notice of the dawn, long before the room showed signs of daylight. My one measly candle swam in a soft puddle of wax with less than three inches of wick left. With watery eyes and a pounding headache, I had to give up trying to see the writing on the pages. Enjoying the little bit of warmth left in the candle, I waited for morning - troubled over what I'd read of Fordham's history.

It was close to an hour before the first sunbeams glinted off the dewdrops in the evergreens and exposed a vision of lacy cobwebs in the window. Minutes later and accompanied by a chorus of chirps and caws, the room was bright with light.

With a weary sigh, I tossed the latest report back in the box and started down the stairs. The guys would soon be waking up and milling around the kitchen table, as if by magic alone, breakfast should appear simply because they had willed it so. Outside, the door on the shed creaked. It sounded like the gang was also looking for breakfast.

I was getting better at building fires. The wood stove in the kitchen was hot by the time Casey came down and I even had a coffee pot ready to perk. He was limping. "Let me look at your leg," I said, motioning for him to sit on a high stool next to the cupboards. I took time to clean the wounds on his leg and replace the bandages. Hopefully, the antiseptic salve I'd found in the medicine cabinet would keep it from becoming infected. "How long do you think this will go on before we actually get to go home?"

"I don't know. We got the house, but they probably found our horses. Soon's we rest up a bit, get our bellies filled, we'll help ourselves to a couple'a mounts and take off. With any luck at all, there won't be no showdown. Unless they force it. I'm damn tired a fighting these assholes." He drew me onto his lap and snuggled his face in my neck. "Did you learn anything last night you didn't already know?"

"Oh, yea. My head's so full of it I can hardly think. Jack says his family had a farm, years ago, downwind from Fordham. He blames all that run off from the production of plutonium, for polluting the soil and their water supply. Evidently, the family lost the farm and their parents died just a few years apart. They were still in their forties. Jack claims the pollution caused their parents' cancer and thyroid disease to the point that it killed them. He feels he has a score to settle."

"Then why take it out on us?"

My weight was obviously hurting Casey's leg. I got up. "They're not, really. From what I can tell, they've been dumping waste illegally in that pit for some time. They were afraid we were from some agency and had come for the express purpose of catching them in the act and putting them in jail. They think we're spies."

"Can't you tell them? That we're just campers, out for a little weekend fun at the lake?"

"I'm trying. But poking some sense into their pencil-pointed heads is going to take some time. They seem to be so taken up with hate and revenge for what happened to their family and the farm, they're not listening."

As Casey moved over to a kitchen chair, his thin hips swaying like a reed in the wind, I was struck by the amount of weight he had lost. Weight he couldn't afford to lose.

"Have some more pancakes while they're hot," I said, flipping a small stack on a plate and setting it down in front of him. "And syrup. There's plenty of syrup." Leaving him to slather them in a pool of sweet maple and warm margarine, I spooned more batter on the hot stovetop and took a few minutes to paw through the pantry. I had no idea what I was looking for, but hoped I'd recognize it before it bit me. It was entirely possible that whoever had hidden that first disk in the rice had been trying to smuggle it out of the house for safe keeping. Although I had an idea the motives were not nearly so pure. In the right hands, there were enough itemized reports, including names and dates, to keep at least one government employee from drawing his five-figured pension and possibly an elected official or two. There could be even more treasures tucked into every nook and cranny, while the culprit awaited his or her chance to abscond with the evidence. Thrusting a hand into the bin of flour, I groped along the bottom and sides, squeezing and stirring, until a white layer covered both myself and the floor. Heavy boots on the stairwell, directly overhead, ended my search and sent me scurrying back to the stove.

It was too late. The bottom of the pancakes had burned to a crisp while the upper half had gelled a sickly white, imbued with crater-like holes along the top. Dropping them into a nearby pail, I replaced them with new spoons of batter and took up my post, spatula at the ready, and waited patiently for them to brown.

The rest of the day was spent heating water and cleaning our clothes and bodies. I had very little time to devote to the files, the reports, or searching the house. Casey volunteered to wash dishes while standing guard over our prisoners. I gratefully accepted the opportunity to bask in a hot tub of water scraping dirt and leaves from my limbs and making sense of the tangled blonde knot atop my head.

On our last escapade at the warehouse, I'd changed into some clean overalls and stuffed my jeans in one of the pockets. With the overalls abandoned in the bottom of a closet and my jeans yet again, soaking in a tub, I needed clean clothes. Although the cotton undies I found in Sister's dresser would suffice, (to me, she'd always be Ranger Woman), her jeans were three sizes too big and the uniforms were out of the question. I picked up a bra by one end — a hefty 3 pounder that could gird a Guernsey cow with room left over to milk. It reminded me of a bad joke my kid brother used to tell about a double barrelled slingshot for bowling balls.

As I looked for a clean pair of socks, a stab of guilt kept me from a more thorough search of her personal effects. *Investigating is one thing. Ransacking a woman's wardrobe was quite another.* I vowed that, other than borrowing a clean set of underclothes, I would stay out. But as I selected a pair of thick cotton knee-highs, I happened to uncover a family Bible.

According to the gold-embossed lettering, it had belonged to their parents. Probably given to them as a wedding present. Just inside the cover, their mother had kept a family tree including the names and birthdates of the last three generations.

I compared them with the notes I'd made from Jimmy's sing-song of months and numbers. He'd been right on every date. Each birth and death was listed on these pages. Except for the parents' death. Up to that time, the mother had been keeping the records updated. But once she died, no one had entered her or the father's death. So how could Jimmy have known it? Or Lorin? And since Jimmy can't read, someone had to tell him the dates. But who? He had no idea what those dates meant. To him, they were simply words and numbers, playing on an endless track in his head.

Making a few more notes on a pad of paper, I continued to read for awhile, finding where the mother had marked her favorite passages. Somehow, I doubted that she would have minded my reading them. In fact, as hard as she had tried to teach her children the Spoken Word, she'd probably approve of my brushing up on spiritual matters and indeed, would have pointed out a verse or two. About an hour later, I thoughtfully smoothed the fragile pages and returned it to the drawer.

Casey had left the bed unmade and in a mess. Oh, well. I should at least straighten it. As I began to smooth the sheets, exhaustion swept over me like I'd been drugged. The next thing I knew, Casey was shaking me awake. He'd fixed dinner hours ago and was insisting that I come down and eat something. I'd slept for a good ten hours.

About midnight, Casey determined it was time he checked up on the thugs outside and hunted down our horses. I was still cleaning up from our simple supper of creamed tuna on instant potatoes and told him about the creaks and groans from the outbuildings in back. "Scrounging food," he said. "Probably slept in the warehouse." At this point, Casey chuckled in irony. "Bet you anything, they even wrapped their asses up in our sleeping bags."

The fact that we'd only used them once before we were run off from our campsite, still rankled. "Well. Nice to know they were warm and toasty," I said, flinging the dish rag in the sink. Because of their little stunts when we first arrived on this mountaintop, we'd spent a number of nights outside in the cold rain. No sleeping bags, no shelter, and barefooted. I sniffled, partly from a head cold I'd picked up and partly from being damned mad.

Casey's plan was to lower himself from the second floor window to the porch roof. From there, he could slide down the supporting post to the ground. As the front door was boarded shut and the back door locked with a dead bolt, it would be too hard for him to sneak out unnoticed if he tried to open either one. It would also prevent the mob from breaking in while he was gone. I was to watch from this same window and on his return, lower him a rope if he needed it.

Inside, the house was unbearably quiet. But the surrounding forest bristled with the sounds of life as I peered out over the porch just far enough to watch for movement on the grassy knoll that served as a back yard. An owl glided over the forest floor, close enough that I could hear the strong flap of his wings and the wild hoot of his mate. A stiff breeze ruffled the evergreens and blew a delicious scent of pine through the stuffy upstairs window.

Downstairs, a loud shatter of glass startled me.

Shit! I forgot about Jimmy. He must have untied Jack. Of course, he would have obeyed the commands of his brother, or sister. Hurriedly, I stuffed a few papers in my coat pocket, the disk and my notes, and tied one end of the rope to a coat rack just inside the window.

Here's hoping he found the horses. I'm ready to get the hell out of this dump. As I shimmied down the rope to the porch roof and made ready to jump, a feeling of having forgotten something gave me reason to pause. Seconds later, a sore reminder of what that was, poked out of the window. Jack had it resting on the windowsill. Another rifle. I'd seen it in the back of Ranger Woman's closet when I was getting dressed. Reacting to my natural aversion to guns, I'd neglected to inform Casey and have him dispose of it.

A number of comments flew through my mind, as I tried to think. To find something to say that would keep his finger off that trigger. *What does one say to a cold-blooded killer, with his gun aimed at the cleavage of your blue work shirt?*

As I watched, he fed shells into the casing and cocked it.

"Jack. Let us go. You've got the upper hand, now. You won. After all we've been through, you can't shoot me now, Jack."

"Who says?"

136

"I do. I say so. You've been through too much, Jack. You survived an incredible ordeal. There's no reason why you should lose it now."

"That's not the way I see it. You been treating me like shit, lady. Swinging your little butt around, all prissy, your nose up in the air. Like you're better than the rest of us. Then come bedtime, back to screwing around with that Casey. I'm tired of it."

"I'm sorry you feel that way. But you can't shoot me now, Jack. It'd be like picking birds off a picket fence. No sport in it, at all."

His mouth twisted behind his beard. "That's easy. I shoot birds all the time. Good target practice."

Thoroughly frightened, I balanced on the edge of the porch roof, wondering if I could jump faster than he could shoot.

The gods were with me that day. Or at least for that moment. Not a half minute later, 'Sis' came up behind Jack and attempted to take the gun away from him. "She's right, Jack," she said. "We may be a lot of things, but we ain't dropped so low that we've begun to shoot people in cold blood, for no reason. Let her go."

"Aw, I wasn't gonna shoot her. Just keep her from takin' off. It ain't fair. She's mine. She even said so, herself. Talked about how much her and I been through together. Didn't you hear her?"

"I said to let her go, Jack. Get yourself a horse and go after them. But we ain't no killers."

"Well, speak for yourself." Wild with anger, Jack swung the butt-end of the rifle at his sister; the only authority figure he'd ever given the time of day. "She's mine, I tell ya." They wrestled in the window, Sis, the stronger and more determined of the two. She jerked it out of his hands, then stiff armed him with one hand while holding the rifle behind her back where he couldn't reach. But Jack had been outwitted, domineered, and browbeat, all his life. He obviously felt it was time to take a stand. "Gimme the gun, Sis. I ain't kidding." He drew himself up and made a mighty lunge for the rifle.

While Sis kept Jack busy, I slid off the edge of the porch roof and dropped to the ground. Quickly, I darted under a large fir, hoping I hadn't been seen yet in a position to watch them fight. In their struggle, the candle I had lit for more light was knocked over. Within minutes, the dingy curtain leaped into flames.

Ranger Woman, or "Sis" as Jack called her, immediately took

137

charge. "Everybody, clear out!", she shouted and snatched the burning curtain from the rods. Jack had disappeared from view, presumably hightailing it down the hall. As I couldn't see the gun, I had to assume Jack had it. Gleefully hefting it in his hot little hands as he raced through the house and out the back door.

The fire had spread to the old cardboard boxes filled with paper. Although I hated to leave Sis to bravely fight the blaze alone, we weren't exactly co-workers. I had to save my own skin before it too, was burnt to a crisp. So, while she stomped and swung her coat at the growing wall of flame, I did little but watch and wait.

The flames quickly engulfed the roof, flashing along the hall-way to the upstairs rooms and spiraled down the staircase. It wouldn't take long before it engulfed the old wooden house. I could no longer see Sis. And though Casey and I had endured a tremendous amount of misery at their hands this last ten days, I had come to know a family that had suffered for at least two generations.

I hoped she was safe.

And that she had saved poor Jimmy.

The barn was on the far side of the house from where I now hid in a grove of pine trees.

Casey would definitely notice the fire, but would he have found the horses?

The forest floor, padded with a century of old pine needles, made for an almost soundless run as I headed for what I hoped was a way home. But even before I got there, I could hear the horses. Their hysterical squeals and kicks at the barn wall.

They smelled smoke.

I crept closer, ready to run should I see one of the mob. Duck-ing under the corral post, I peered into the barn. No one was present, not even the truck drivers. Evidently, all hands had been called to the burning house. The horses were terrified, milling around in their stalls, snorting and pawing at the barn floor. A large brownish-black stallion, one I recognized as Sis's mount, eyed me at the door. He reared, rolling his eyes and tossing his fine head. A quick scan of the other stalls, told me that my bay was not there.

My presence in the barn enraged the stallion. As if to warn me not to come even one step closer, he struck his stall with one sharp hoof, drew back his lips in exhibit of brown teeth, and neighed at me.

No problem, horsey. I'd spend the rest my life in these woods, living like a hermit if need be, before I approached you.

Smoke from the house poured from the doors and windows. As far as I could tell, the barn was not yet burning. But it wouldn't be long before the sparks reached the old cedar roof or possibly a scattering of hay.

The horses squealed in panic. And well they should. If the barn went up, they'd be burnt to cinders. I had to let them out, give them a chance to run for their lives. Throwing open the barn door, I ran along the stalls, opening each gate, expecting them to bolt.

But they didn't. Instead, they milled around in circles, bumping and pawing one another. "Shoo, horses. Go on. Get out of here."

They wouldn't leave the shelter of the barn.

Lastly, I released the spring on the stallion's stall and ducked around behind, keeping the open gate between him and me and giving him a clear, straight path to the outside door. Hopefully, he would lead them out. Instead, he proceeded to bite each rump he could reach and whack them with his strong neck.

But he too, refused to leave.

This is not going to work. Someone with more horse sense than I would have to deal with these animals.

Leaving all the gates and doors open, I dashed outside and headed down to Casey's and my old meeting place. The same place where we had been going to meet after the warehouse incident and where Casey had kept the horses tied. Sneaking through the shrubs and under sweet-smelling pine boughs, the smoke had not yet reached them, I stopped to cough up some bad stuff from my lungs and draw in huge amounts of clean, fresh, oxygen-laden air. Careful not to be seen, I kept to the tall trees until I was out of hearing distance. Then raced as fast as possible considering the darkness of the path.

I could have saved the trip. No Casey. Or horses, either one. Behind me, the house was being engulfed in flames. More smoke and wilder squeals suggested that the barn was also now on fire. I crept back, popped under the branch, and sat down in my old hidyhole under the huge cedar. Evidently, the crew had given up on saving the house and had moved to the barn, hoping to save the horses. I could hear their hoarse shouts as they tried to lead them, one at a time, out of the smoke.

I waited under the tree, shivering, watching the walls of the house crumble as flames streamed from the windows. Out of sight of my little den but not out of hearing range, the anguished scream of horses being burnt by the raging fire shook me to my toes. Never before, had I felt so helpless. It was incredible, but the horses didn't seem to understand that the barn was burning down and would no longer provide shelter.

They needed to escape.

Or they'd go down with it.

Suddenly, a short figure dashed from the yard and into the burning front door of the house.

Jimmy!

Peering through the cedar boughs, I watched for a moment thinking that his sister or at least Jack, would call him back. But no one seemed to notice. Evidently, they were too busy with the burning barn and the horses. Too late, I shouted as loud as I dared, "Jimmy. Don't go in there. WAIT."

The flames were now on the roof. The staircase and even the walls would not hold up much longer. He was already inside.

Poor Jimmy was trapped.

I dashed to the front porch, peering up the smoke-clogged stairway. Again, I called. "Jimmy! Come back. Don't go up there."

The only sounds were the whoosh the fire made and his hard footsteps on the top of the stairs, racing down the hall.

One last time, I looked down the trail to the barn and the outlying woods, hoping some member of his family would miss him and figure out where he had gone.

But the only one I could see, was Casey. He was running for all he was worth, up the hill from the area of the warehouse. He didn't see me. He was making tracks for the barn, determined to save the horses from certain death.

There was only one thing left to do. Taking several deep breaths and arranging my jacket's hood over my hair, I darted in through the door and up the stairs.

Chapter

16

Jimmy was not in his room.

Wasting precious seconds, I dashed in, coughing and calling his name through the smoke, and even looked in his closet. He wasn't there.

Ohmigod. Let him be in Sister's room. Please. There's not time to be looking for him all over the upstairs.

Whisking down the hall, I swung a left at the landing and bounded past the storage closets. Ranger Woman's room was in the farthest end of the hallway, stuffy with the windows closed and little if any draft. The smoke there was mostly filtered like a light haze. I rushed in the room and found Jimmy pawing through his sister's dresser.

I believed I knew what he was looking for.

It was very dark and we were totally dependent on my sense of touch and memory of what had been in that dresser and where to find it. Quickly, I fumbled along the front, jerked open the small drawer in the center, and pulled out the family Bible. I placed his hands on it, promising we'd take it with us and insisting we leave this room and the house before it was too late. But he was still not happy. He continued to paw at the clothes, hysterically crying and coughing, wailing his favorite tune, "Jesus loves me, yes I know . . . "

Perhaps . . . in the back in the same drawer, I pulled out another book I'd seen when I first found the Bible. Older and even more worn. He cried out in glee and clasped it to his chest, just above his heart. Jimmy had found his mother's old gospel and prayer book with all the tunes and words to his favorite songs.

Letting him hold it, I grabbed his other hand and pulled him down the stairs, forcing him to take them two at a time. Outside, I continued to pull him deep into the woods, far enough to breath good air. Finally, in a small meadow we sank to the ground, letting the damp grass cool our hot cheeks.

His sister had seen us. Minutes later she charged down the path. "Jimmy! Are you hurt? Did you get burned?" She ran to him, ignoring me, and hugged him around the neck. "Don't ever run off like that, again. You scared the devil out of me." After checking him over, looking to see if he'd been badly burnt and finding only some singed eyebrows and smoke-blackened lips, she turned to me.

Offering me her hand, Sis helped me get up off the ground. As I stood on rubbery legs, she fixed me with a riveting green-eyed gaze that made me feel she could read my mind like a blackboard. "I saw what you did," she said, " . . . running in the house. I didn't know you'd gone in after Jimmy. I thought you were after some of those silly reports. Until I saw you both come out. Then I knew you'd saved his life. There's no way I can ever thank you."

Wincing under her strong grip, I mumbled something about being glad he was all right and motioned to a log lying next to the path. We sat on it, Jimmy, Ranger Woman and I in a kind of truce, happy to be alive. I was too exhausted to speak or do little more than breathe huge quantities of fresh air and occasionally cough up a grey-streaked phlegm.

Although I would have traded anything I owned for a nap, after about a half an hour, I began to recover my senses. On the side where she couldn't see, I flexed the fingers of my right hand, still smarting from her so-called 'handshake' and wondered if she'd done permanent damage.

It was then I noticed that she too, looked a little green around the gills. As she passed a hand over her face and neck, her head drooping almost to her knees, I took a chance and said, "Look. I think it's really time we stopped being at odds with each other and started cooperating. I've found out quite a bit about your predicament. And yes, I know about the illegal dumping. But . . . I think I can also answer some of your questions about your parents. Not now, but you and I will need to talk."

To my surprise, she nodded and gave me a long, sideways squint. "You're probably right."

"Not just 'probably', Sis. I am right, and I think you know it."

She lurched a little at my use of her family nickname and bestowed me with another of her penetrating glares. But she was smart enough to know I had a point. "You've got a deal. What's your name?"

"Kathy."

"OK, Kathy. I won't promise you I'll agree or go along with anyone else's schemes. But . . . I am willing to talk. And because you saved Jimmy's life, I'll try to return the favor, deed for deed." Thrusting up and out her ample bosom with a straight-backed pride, she leveled her first finger at me and said, "I, personally, will not try to harm you or your friend, nor will I try to keep you from leaving these mountains. When you're ready to go, that is."

Head reeling from this new pronouncement, I again let her crush my hand in her absurd idea of a handshake. As the tiny bones in my palm crunched like Shredded Wheat under her steel-like grasp, I wondered where Casey was and if he would hear me if I called. With my frustration level well over the boiling point, I wanted to scream and cuss and cry and kick someone, all at the same time. If I had the energy. But mostly, I wanted to shout to the tree-tops that we could go home now.

Sister said.

After awhile, we trudged up the path, arm in arm, supporting and consoling, knowing that whatever it was, it was over.

The house was gone, a rumble of charred logs and half-burnt furniture. In the area where the kitchen once stood, the two truck drivers tramped through the smoky ruins, grumbling and looking for God-knows-what. Momentarily, they gawked at the three of us, then shrugged and returned to their search. Evidently they were beyond being shocked.

Instead, they had focused on the basic parts of life such as finding enough food for a quick meal and probably the keys to the truck. As I drew close enough to overhear some of their gripes, I realized that there was indeed, more to worry about than the actions of two unpredictable women.

The smell of the smoke and burning wallpaper was bad. But it wasn't the worst part. The likelihood of smoldering embers setting fire to the woods was a dreadful possibility. The gas tank that fueled the generator had caught a spark and blown like a big bomb. Without it, we had no pump with which to draw water. And without water, we were all at the mercy of Mother Nature's whims. It was a miracle that we were not running for our lives this very moment, trying to outdistance a raging forest fire.

To complicate matters even farther, the radio that Ranger Woman would have reported the fire with had been destroyed with the house. They'd have to depend on the occasional fly-by of a Forest Service helicopter to spot the smoke. And somehow, with the man-made pit never having been detected, I sensed that Ranger Woman pretty much called the shots. Which meant, that unless she'd ordered it beforehand, I doubted that a helicopter would dare venture over to this part of the mountain.

We were on our own.

Half of the barn was also gone, but the men had managed to save the horses' feed and the room that held the tack - an assortment of bridles and saddles and horse blankets. They had not been harmed.

For once, it was a picture I didn't want to take. A scene I'd rather forget than keep for posterity. But, this entire story, even though I had experienced it, seen it, felt it, and smelled it, would seem, within a few weeks, like a bad dream. And if it was that hard to me to assimilate, it would be difficult, to say the least, for the authorities to believe.

I had to have absolute proof.

When Ranger Woman wasn't looking, I popped under the old cedar tree branch, poked the camera's lens through an opening between the leaves, and began to snap some fairly complete shots. Using my close-up lens, I managed to get some shots of her and the truck drivers pawing through the burnt rumble. When I'd finished, I crawled out the back of the hidyhole and repeated the same process at the barn. It was empty of horses and men and I had a free hand to finish capturing on film, my moment in history. A moment that, given the circumstances, not everyone would want to admit.

As far as I could tell, none of the Gillespie family knew about my picture taking and I hoped to keep it that way. Careful not to be seen, I snuck back to the big cedar and rehid the camera in its branches.

At dusk, Ranger Woman broke into the shed and disbursed what food was left. She then directed the men to bring Casey's and my sleeping bags to the tack room in what was left of the barn. She and I would sleep there. That finished, she waved them off to the bunkhouse. Luckily, it was far enough away that the fire had not touched it.

Yet.

The smell of smoke threatened to overpower us until we managed to prop open some windows and doors and get a good draft going through. Ranger Woman and I cleared the little room of straw and dusty gunny sacks, anything that could catch a stray spark, then settled in for the night. And while we tried not to be distracted by the crash of an occasional beam from the still smoldering house or the squeal and nicker of a nearby horse, we were both, very obviously, uncomfortable. I still hadn't seen hide nor hair of Casey, and Jack had literally disappeared. Jimmy refused to stay with the men in the bunkhouse, so we bedded him down with us on a layer of horse blankets and the three of us sang a few old hymns to help him go to sleep.

It was time Ranger Woman and I joined forces and compared notes. To start the conversation off on the right foot, I dug into my jacket and handed her the family Bible. "Here," I said. "I thought you might want to keep this. That and Jimmy's song book was all I managed to save from the fire. I wish I could have gotten more."

She was astonished. "Oh," she said, and clutched the Bible to her chest. "Thank you. So very much. I . . . how will I ever repay you?" Silently, she began to cry, hugging the Bible and rocking gently back and forth. "I'm sorry. It's just that, this means so much to us . . ." She gazed at me with sad, wet eyes. "It's all we have left of Mamma. She used to read to us, every night. Kind of like our own little prayer meeting. And then we'd sing from the song book. All the old gospels."

"Well, uh, you really should thank Jimmy. He, actually, when he ran upstairs . . ."

" . . . and you saved his life, too. I don't know what to say."

"To begin with, you can talk to me. Tell me what is going on with that pit, the bins of nuclear waste, the dead cowboy, and why the hell did you disable my car and then come shooting at us?"

At least she had the decency to look guilty. "We thought you were there as an agent from the National Forest Service, posing as a tourist. A spy, hired to investigate us. Actually, all I ordered was a search of your car and the removal of any briefcases, papers, letters, anything that would tell us who you were. And guns. We couldn't permit you to have any weapons here on the compound. The rest of that burglarizing; your tent, sleeping bags and boots, all your uh, personal items, was all Jack's idea. I didn't even know about it until much later."

"My personal items? What personal items?"

"Jack has, uh, an array of your, shall we say, sort of scanty things? I caught him once, in his room. He had them all laid out on his bedspread, admiring the lacy stuff and little bows. Uh . . ." With a sniff, she drew herself up, smug and self-righteous. "We had words about it, him and I. About proper Christian behavior for a young man. Told him he'd have to give them up. He wouldn't. He threw an awful temper tantrum and went running out of the house. Stayed out for three or four days. Probably camped up at an old line cabin, away up the Sauk River."

This family's way of retreating into religious doctrine any time they were pressed, was more than interesting. It was infuriating. And definitely designed to throw me off by making me feel inferior. Heathenistic. Only a godless pagan would dare interrogate such Pious People Of The Cloth.

I wasn't buying it. "Then maybe you'll tell me why you killed that cowboy."

She blanched. "What? You think it was me . . .? Dear Lord, I never would have . . . Johnny and I were in love. We were to be married as soon as we could find a pastor of our own faith. We thought it was you or your . . . uh, boyfriend that, uh . . ."

This time it was my turn. "My boyfriend, as you call him, is actually my fiance. This innocent camping trip . . ."

"You're kidding. You and Casey? Getting married?"

Seizing the moment, I too, drew myself up in a huff. "Oh yes, that was only the reason we came up here. Before we got lost in a downpour of rain. To enjoy a weekend away from the noisy city. Commune with God's natural wonders in celebration of our en-

146

gagement." Although I'd never be able to reach her dimensions in pure thrust, I allowed my small shapely breasts to point to a higher creed in unrestrained dignity. "We never supposed the forest would be trashed and all the wildlife destroyed."

Withstanding her green-eyed scowl, I expertly brought us back to the subject at hand. "So. If you didn't shoot him, and neither did we, who did? Someone had to. Was Jack on another one of his nightly prowls?"

"My brother never left the house until after you people showed up."

"Are you certain of that? Would you testify to that in court? Swear to it on a stack of Bibles?"

"Yes. Anytime." She placed her right hand on her mother's Good Book, and said, "I'll swear to it now. There was not a single morning that Jack was not in his room where he belonged until after my employees spotted your car."

"That's not what I asked. Can you verify that Jack never left the house? On a fast horse and good knowledge of the trail, he could have popped out the office window, the same way I did, gone galloping through the night creating chaos, and easily been back by morning."

"Of course not, since you put it that way. But then you're still barking up the wrong tree." She curled herself up on the sleeping bag, sulking. I wanted to ask about the employees, but she seemed to have more to say about little brother. "Jack always liked Johnny. In fact, Johnny had promised to bring him some things on his return trip. Men's magazines and such. He was great about talking to Jack about . . . matters that men . . . talk about. Like a father would, or an older brother. Jack could hardly wait for Johnny to go this last time." She shrugged one rounded shoulder with an honest sadness. "The earlier he left, the sooner he'd be back."

"All right. We'll let Jack be for awhile. How about those two truck drivers?"

"I have no idea. As long as they're ready for work when they're supposed to be, I don't even try to keep up with their nightly visits. There's no reason why they would want to hurt Johnny as far as I know, but I suppose anything's possible."

I liked Janice, or at least was learning to . . . but had a hard time believing she was the brains behind the nuclear waste scheme and could run the whole operation and take care of Jimmy, with only two hired hands and a schizo brother. No way.

She was leaving something out. Something important.

"By the way, what date did your parents die?"

"Oh. Some years ago, when I was still in high school. Why?"

"I mean, can you tell me the exact date. Day, month, and year, that they died?"

"No. Not without going to the courthouse to look it up. I might be able to figure out the year by how old the twins were, but that's about it. It's not something I like to think about any more than I have to."

"Then there's only one left. Jack's pal, the one with the weeks growth of whiskers."

Head bent, she dusted some imaginary lint from her uniform pants. "I was wondering if you'd run into him yet. His name is Loren. He's a doctor. We dated for awhile over in Eastern Washington. In the Tri-cities area. The boys and I had just lost our parents and the farm. I was trying to find a job and keep what was left of our family, together. We were having a really tough time of it when Loren and I met. He got me my first position with the Forest Service and moved us into this house. When things didn't work out between us, he left."

Chin up and boobs on the rise, she was back on the track of sainthood. "Kinda stormed out, when I insisted on the sanctity of marriage. BEFORE we could consummate."

At this rate, she'd soon be claiming to have regrown a maidenhead.

"I had an idea he was still hanging around," she continued. "I'd see some evidence of it now and then. He broke into the warehouse a couple of times, knew exactly what he was looking for. Climbed into the house and pilfered some things out of the office, while I slept in the very next room. That kind of thing. But I actually haven't seen him since he tried to lure me into a life of sin."

I was getting used to her occasional side-steps into religion. And even better at keeping us on course.

"What kind of doctor was he?"

"Not a purely medical doctor, you know. Like the kind who'd set your leg if you broke it or give you some pills for an earache.

148

He's a scientist. Terribly well educated. All kinds of degrees from the universities. He used to work for Fordham, but then they got this younger man and didn't need Loren anymore. Some genius, college graduate from the University of Washington."

"So, he's the one that got you started. And supplied the nuclear waste material, too."

"Yes. I won't lie to you. Loren had connections. That computer upstairs, well at least the one that had been upstairs, was his. He used it then, for National Security. Keeping the Russians at bay. That sort of thing."

"In other words, he built bombs. Atomic, nuclear bombs in the 60s."

She sniffed. "To protect our country from the Communists. If it wasn't for him, democracy as we know it would be a thing of the past." Her shirt front quivered, placing a whole row of buttons and the fabric they were sewn on, under severe stress.

I was getting real tired of her. "Oh, come on. You don't know that. You're just repeating some rhetoric you heard somewhere along the way. The guy got you a great job, a free place to live in addition to keeping Jack away from all civilized societies, an obviously wise and necessary choice, plus he helped you make a whole bunch of money. Looks to me like he probably earned a quick roll in the hay. Then, when you thought you had the whole scheme down pat and didn't need him anymore, old Pops got the boot."

"Really, Kathy. I don't know how you were raised, but Mamma always taught us to do right. Live by the Ten Commandments. Walk the Straight and Narrow Path. That sort of thing."

"Leave my mother out of this!" She may never know how close I was to losing my cool. "Talk about your own Mom all you want. But not mine." I was noticeably shaking and absolutely furious. With great self-control and a deep breath, I beat down the urge to slap her silly and forced myself to get back to the issue at hand. "Now, where were we? Where did this Doctor Loren go, after he left your house?"

She seemed to think it was funny. "Oh, no. I thought you knew." She clucked her tongue, her hand flying up to rest on one cheek, and made a show of trying not to giggle. "His name wasn't Dr. Loren. That's his first name. His full name is Doctor Loren Robb. And I have no idea where he went after our break-up. Johnny and I started seeing each other shortly after that, and I simply picked myself up and went on with my life."

Dr. Robb! The same one who wrote those reports on the disk. *Oh, my. He was the doctor who performed the experiments.* Could she actually be this much in the dark about the good doctor? I doubted it. But then, why is she protecting him? Maybe she thinks she's protecting herself. And the twins. And then, maybe I'm wrong. It was the cowboy who had the disk. And that disk was the only place I had seen where the dates of the parents' death was mentioned. Who else, besides Loren, knew enough about old military computers and had the ability to be in a position at the right time and place to program in a password? I was trying to digest the new revelations when a clomp of boot outside the door, startled us both out of our skins.

"Casey! Where have you been?"

"Taking care of things. Rounding up the horses." With a longer than usual look at Ranger Woman, which included a full review of her cleavage, he turned to me and said, "Come morning, you and I are ready to go."

"Good. I'm glad you're here. Our friend the forest ranger was just telling us about Dr. Robb. The one you and I affectionately called Whiskers."

"What about him?"

"He seems to be the one who stands out as a suspect to have killed that cowboy. I was just going to inform her that Dr. Robb is no longer with us." I paused for full effect, knowing it was wrong to gloat but, nevertheless, enjoying every bit of it. "We have good reason to believe he's gone to his just rewards. The Creator has called him home."

"Loren is dead, too?" It was her turn to be dismayed. "How did it happen?"

I glanced at Casey, hoping to catch his eye and warn him to be careful of not revealing too much at this time. "We won't go into that just now, but it comes, so to speak, from the horses' mouth."

But Casey was too intent on keeping the record straight. He interrupted. "Now, Kathy. Don't go telling tales out of school. We don't know what happened to this doctor. If he's dead, or what."

150

Luckily, he had leaned his head back, resting it on a corner of my sleeping bag. I gouged him with a thumbnail, whispering into his ear. "But, you just said the other day . . ."

He answered quietly. "I said I left him for dead. But, while I was chasing horses, I went back to the creek where I left him. He's long gone. And not to his maker, either. No sign of him there. No body, no nothing. You say the guy was a doctor, he must have patched hisself up and hightailed it."

Ranger Woman hadn't been listening to Casey and me. She was still working through the idea that yet another lover had died. "I can't believe Loren's dead," she said, hunching her shoulders and drawing herself in. The news had hit home. She was trembling.

Taking a chance, I grasped her arms and gave her a mighty shake. "Janice, I know you've got a brain in there. Somewhere. You've got to think this whole thing through. How would Dr. Robb have known the exact dates of your parents' death? And why would those dates have made such an impact that he used them as part of the password into his private computer files? In fact, that password is made up from the dates of every important event your family has ever experienced. Every birth, and death, and whatever else happened, is there."

I snatched a roll of old paper out from under my jacket and shoved it under her nose. "Look at this. It's a report on some of those experiments. Your father's name is mentioned right here." I jabbed a finger at a particular line and almost forced her to read it. "See? It's an agenda. A report showing who's expected to be going up before the board that day. Isn't that your Dad's name? In an earlier paper I read last night, there were references to putting him on probation for not cooperating. Do you remember hearing about any arm-twisting tactics? Did your father really volunteer to take all those shots? Or was he blackmailed?"

She gaped at me. "It's hard to remember," she said, comprehension beginning to dawn and with it the horror of its meaning. "There was one night that . . . kind of stands out. Daddy hardly ever argued with Mamma, but this time he did. Got real upset. It was late and the loud voices scared me. Woke me up. Daddy was banging on the table shouting that we needed money. I was about six years old. I know Mamma was already pregnant with the boys then, and she was begging him not to do anymore experiments.

Said they'd turned him into a guinea pig. Daddy was probably worried about keeping his job. They'd have lost Mamma's medical insurance for sure . . . and I remember something about Daddy getting paid extra when he 'volunteered' his services. We didn't know . . ." She'd begun to weep, and, I felt, to get honest. "Just like I didn't know Loren had actually worked on one of the projects. At the time, he hid the information somewhere, scared he'd be found out that he hadn't followed certain guidelines. He was a private contractor, doing some tests. That's the reason I broke up with him. You're darn right I have a brain. I figured it out. About Loren. Couldn't handle the idea that he was the one did this to Jimmy.

I hated having to remind Janice of her family's painful past. But I couldn't see any way of getting around it. And it would have to happen now while she seemed willing to open up. I might never have this opportunity again. "Uhm, Janice, in that Bible you're holding, there's a family tree. Your mother had entered another name."

"Yes. Baby Jessica." Sobbing openly, she banged a fist on one knee. "I was supposed to have a sister, you know. A twin sister. But she didn't make it. She was stillborn. Loren and his cronies down there at Fordham took all that away from me. They weren't satisfied to pump the radioactive junk downriver and blow it out the smokestacks. No. They had to do this other . . . these things, to Daddy. You've got to believe me, I didn't know. He swore he was never really involved in that . . . said he just studied lab rats and took samples in the fields. To protect humanity. Operated on sick sheep. That kind of thing. Had I known, that he was the one who put the radiation to Daddy's . . . (sob) you know, I forget the medical term for a mans' whatchamacallit."

"Reproductive organs."

"Yea. My Dad's reproductive organs was cooked by Doctor Loren Robb. Then, they threatened to fire Daddy if he wouldn't go through with more tests. Had I known at the time when he and I were . . . still sharing the same bed . . . I'd a had to do some real damage to that man. In a place where he wouldn't hardly forget what he did to our father, if you know what I mean."

"Yes. I do believe I know what you mean. And to tell you the truth, I wouldn't have blamed you a bit."

Her hands fluttered like small birds. "Talking about it, really

... sort of ... brings back a lot of things I don't like to think about. And now that Loren's gone too, I . . ."

Casey could not stand it. He had to put the facts straight. "Look. I just said, the guy ain't dead, after all. I thought he was, but he ain't."

I nudged Casey as a reminder not to interrupt. But by the look in her murky green eyes, this time, Janice had definitely heard him. "I'm sure it does hurt. You were just a little girl. And I do thank you for your honesty. Your Mamma would be proud." I let that settle for a minute, thinking it through. But something was still nagging at me. She'd never seen the disk, in fact could care less about it, and had shown no inclination to read any of the boxes of reports. "I appreciate your help, Janice. Very much. And for having to recall some very private family matters. But, how did you ever find out about Loren?"

"How?" She wiped her nose on her sleeve, trying to compose herself. "Oh. Well, Johnny told me. You know, the guy you call the `cowboy'? He pointed it out one night. Showed how it was right there, in black and white. Some of those reports, just like the ones you got."

Chapter

17

That was the next question. Who exactly was this cowboy? All I knew was that he'd been Ranger Woman's last lover. Where were his remains? The things from his pockets? Did Casey retrieve the stuff from his saddle bags? Could anything be retrieved from the smoking ruins? What was the link between the cowboy and the disk? Did he know he was packing it out? If not, who else could have put it in the box of instant rice?

It was all making my head hurt. I snuggled down into the sleeping bag, ready to go to sleep. Ranger Woman was tending to Jimmy. He'd been muttering in his sleep, probably from a bad dream. I told her good night, then reached over to give Casey's arm an affectionate rub.

"Go on to sleep," he said, for once allowing himself to show emotion. He brushed a wad of curls out of my eyes with a great tenderness and kissed my forehead. "Come morning, we're getting the hell off this mountaintop and going home. I got the horses hid, along with all our gear, and plenty of food to last us till we reach town. Nothing can stop us now. Nothing."

"Sounds great. And we'll go, too. Just as soon as we get back from that line cabin."

Casey closed his eyes in an obvious attempt to humor me and began to chew on a wisp of straw. I could see him thinking, almost out loud. *Isn't that just like a woman. Always have to explain things twice.* "No, Kathy. I told you now, I already been there," he said, working his straw through the caverns of his teeth, scooping out a molar. "Don't need to go back. Now, I got all our stuff packed and ready to go. The horses been fed and watered, and come first light, we're heading home."

Knowing I'd never be able to convince him that his attitude was belittling to me, I adopted the same tone and made a show of patting his other hand. "But Casey darlin', don't you understand? We still don't know anything about this cowboy who got killed. Other than his name was Johnny. Or at least, that's what he told Ra . . . I mean, Janice." I chuckled, knowing I'd almost called her by her nickname, imagining the look on her face if I did, and wondering what Bible verse the moniker `Ranger Woman' would produce.

But Casey thought I was laughing at him. He flung his piece of straw to the floor. "Damn it, Kathy. You been bitching about going home for what, two weeks now? Almost two weeks. I know I got damn tired of hearing it. And now, you say you want to take a little side trip?"

"Casey, we've got to have that information. If we wait and trust some sheriff or whatever to come up here and look for any evidence, you might as well hang it up. They won't have any idea of what to look for and you know as well as I do, they're not going to listen to us. You'll be their prime suspect. They could pin that homicide on you as well as on anybody else and who'd be the wiser? Do you have the money for a decent defense attorney? And I'm talking top dollar. Don't look to Darrian for any help. He hates murder trials. We've got to go, Casey. Or whatever's there will be gone."

"And I say, no. Going up there, ransacking the damn place, that'll take all of a day. Figure two more to go up and back, that's three more days. Shot. No, Kathy. We're going home. And that's it. I said all I'm going to about the whole damn shit'nkaboodle."

"Then let me put it this way, Casey. I'm going. Alone, if I have to. With Janice, if she'll come. But I'm going."

It was the worst argument we'd ever had. Ranger Woman finally had to interrupt. "Look, you two. Tone it down a little. You're waking Jimmy up. Kathy, you want to go up there? I'll go with you." She folded her arms at the midriff, causing her shirt

156

button to come undone and all that inside to jiggle.

Casey stared.

I cleared my throat and kicked him in the shins.

"Casey," she said, pretending not to notice. "You're welcome to come with us or head for town. Whatever you want is fine with me. Plus, I been thinking about what you said, Kathy. And I got to know about Loren. For sure. What in the world was he thinking when he did that . . . experiment on Daddy's . . . organs. And did he have anything to do with Johnny's death. If he was the one, I swear, he won't get away with it."

But Casey was not into the hunt. He was ready to go home. "We can come back and do all that. And bring somebody who knows what the hell to do with these apes if we catch them. Somebody who can legally arrest people and shut this damn hole down."

Ranger Woman hadn't heard a word Casey said. " . . . and it wouldn't hurt to see if Jack's up there. He can be awful mean and God only knows what he's got up his sleeve this time. When Jack gets like this, there's no stopping him. You know, Casey . . . he could very well be sitting down the road, waiting for you two to ride by. And you wouldn't even know it till you felt a bullet in the back. By then, it'd be too late for you and for Kathy. He's got his mind set on her and believe me, he ain't gonna let up until he gets what he wants. Might take weeks, years even. But you better believe, he'll find a way. And it won't be nice."

It was two against one. Casey would be taking us to the line cabin, like it or not. With clenched jaw and glittering eyes, he twisted around and thumped his shoulder onto the horse blanket hard enough to bounce. He then covered himself with one corner and turned to the wall.

By morning, Casey had recovered his pride, but he wasn't talking. I didn't bother to try. He went after the horses without being asked and the three of us packed up to leave.

After much mothering and order-giving, Janice left Jimmy with the truck drivers.

The ride up to the line cabin was through some of the prettiest parts of the Cascade Mountains. I'd never really noticed the wild rhododendron bushes, never having seen them before in full bloom. But many of them we passed had grown, year after year, supported by the branches of the evergreens and were almost as tall. Several times, a turn in the trail had stopped us in our tracks. I was astonished to find that the huge bundles of soft pink blossoms actually grew that high. "Oh, aren't they beautiful?" I said, feeling a fullness in my heart that hadn't been there before.

Janice answered, reining her horse up alongside of mine. "Yes, they are. Usually, they'll bloom a lot earlier in the year but up this high and in the shade of that overhang, there'll be snow here on the ground until almost May." She pointed to a rock wall of craggy peaks that rose up above us.

It was an awesome sight. And I would have enjoyed it more had Casey not been acting like such a poop.

It was late that day when we arrived. Janice, I could not help but think of her as Ranger Woman, wanted to ride directly up to the cabin and confront Jack, if he was there, with all the diplomacy of a bulldozer. Casey insisted we survey the place first, in order to have some idea of what we were walking into. I had to agree with him. "We better listen to Casey," I said, watching him out of the corner of my eye. "Let him nose around a little. We don't know who's there, if its Jack or some drifter."

All this while, Casey had been combing his hair with his fingers and positioning his hat to set just right, tipping it at a roguish angle. That done, he cast me a sideways glance and gave me a wink. I smiled, my heart already beginning to melt. "We'll wait here for you."

As always, he headed first for the barn. He'd check it to see how many horses were there and if they'd been ridden recently. None of us had any idea his excursion would turn out to be that bad.

It was getting dark and cold. On our last nocturnal ride, Casey had taught me how to get warm. Get down, out of the wind, nestle in the crook of my horses' neck and shoulder, and hug him. His steamy warmth not only kept me from freezing, but proved to be extremely comforting.

After about an hour, Ranger Woman was pacing. "He ain't coming, Kathy," she said, nervously slapping the bridle reins against her thigh. Her horse fidgeted, tried backing away. "And we can't stay out here all night."

Well, that was just fine and dandy for her to say. She had nothing to fear either from little brother or exboyfriend. But I was scared. Scared of staying here, scared of going back, and scared of what I'd done to Casey. His life could very well be hanging in the balance, and it was I who made it so. And since there was no way I would leave without Casey, there was only one other tactic. "We'll have to go in after him."

"What's this 'we' shit? I ain't going in there." So. Jack wasn't the only one to react under pressure with a filthy mouth. Evidently, confronted by the hazards of the dark night and the risk to her own life and limb, Ranger Woman's call to Christendom had been kissed off. She jerked the reins from the branch where they'd been tied and mounted her horse. "It's just like I told you. You never know what Jack's gonna do. He has no conscience. At all. And, if he's got his dither up . . . its anybody's guess who he might shoot. Including me. I'm sorry about your friend, but I ain't going in there. Not now."

I'd have given anything for a real smart remark, something snappy that conveyed my anger and disappointment. But all I could think of was, "Do unto others as you would have them do unto you."

As she turned her horse towards the trail, she said, with as much heart as a clod of ground, "God takes care of those who take care of themselves."

Something had been bothering me for some time. Ranger Woman knew I'd be turning her in for running an illegal nuclear waste dump the minute I got back to town. And yet she hadn't even tried to make a deal. In fact, she'd wanted to be all palsy-walsy. Claimed that the saving of Jimmy's life, had earned me the right to leave this mountaintop whenever I wanted. But did she have the fortitude to follow through on that commitment? Or any others, for that matter. "And what about your friend, Loren? This big need you had to find out about he and your Daddy? And, besides, you already knew what Jack was like before we rode up here and put Casey in danger. Remember? You told us yourself just a few hours ago."

Her eyes narrowed and her lips curled. "Loren ain't there. If he was, and he heard that I was out here, he'd be on his way to my side this very minute. And to hell with anyone tried to stop him, including Jack."

As her horse stomped and snorted, reacting to the punishing pull on the reins that kept him from bolting towards home, I was struck by my horse's reaction. He nosed me under the arm, shoving me ahead a few steps, as if to remind me that he was there and if it was time to go then maybe I best climb on.

I was also struck by a feeling of deja' vu. I was about to walk into that cabin, relive the horrors of being kept hostage by Jack, only this time we'd be pelted by Ranger Woman's occasional forays into Scripture.

No, thanks.

I climbed up into the saddle and was immediately glad. It not only reduced my feeling of vulnerability but gave me a much better range of vision. I could see over the tops of the bushes and all the way to the cabin.

Ranger Woman didn't much like it. "Well, Miss High and Mighty. Where ya think you're going? What happened to all your bright ideas about going in after that great lover of yours, Casey? If you ask me, you could have done better."

I didn't answer. I was too busy watching a small light approach. A creepy feeling scampered up my spine as the tiny beam left the area of the cabin door, weaving and bobbing up and down.

It was coming this way.

It was a flashlight.

Chapter

18

It was an eerie night with clouds that came and went, harboring the full-moon behind them. The dark had a maroonish, almost red cast to it and the little bit of light carried in some man's hand was disturbing, to say the least.

Who was it, behind that flashlight? My boyfriend or hers? The man who would save my life or the man who would take it. I was no longer sure, which was which.

I reached down and grabbed the reins of Casey's horse. Ranger Woman didn't say anything, but I sensed she didn't like it, felt her hate and anger. For some reason, she was no longer that eager to go home. In fact, she seemed more inclined to stick around so she could monitor me.

The one with the flashlight was getting closer. There was something familiar about that swinging and loose-legged walk, but there was something different, too . . . Still a good 50 yards off, I was almost certain I recognized . . .

Casey. With a whoop and a holler, I gouged my horse in the flanks. He sprang into action and within three bounds, I knew what it was that was bothering me. There was more than one man behind that flashlight.

The other man saw me coming and began to run. I reined the horse close to Casey and threw him his horses' reins. Then, without even slowing down, I tried bashing my horse's shoulder into Loren. He jumped out of the way, and I missed. Damn it! What happened to those horses that could turn on a dime? It took me a good minute to slow my horse down, let alone make him go back the other way.

By now, Casey had mounted his horse and was galloping towards Ranger Woman. She had dismounted and was running, bouncy-boobs and red hair flying, towards the fleeing Whiskers. "Shoot him you fool! Get the girl, too."

Shots rang out. Something buzzed close enough to my ear that I felt the wind as it went by. We spurred our horses for the trees. More shots. Casey's horse stumbled and rolled.

Ohmigod. They shot at Casey and hit his horse! My horse was within three bounds to safety behind the trees. But I'd forced Casey into this mess and I couldn't cop out on him, now. I reined my horse in, although he was close to full stride and didn't want to stop.

In the background, Ranger Woman's voice carried across the small clearing. "He's down. Tie him up and I'll go after the girl. That little bitch has paraded around this place long enough."

I pulled up, preparing to in after Casey. But somewhere from the dark of night he saw me, knew me well enough to know what I'd do, and hollered, "Go, Kathy. GO. ITS A TRAP."

He was right, of course. I couldn't help him or anyone else once they got their hands on me. I dug my horse in the flanks, felt his mighty leap to the trail. He'd also been right about going for the Sheriff. We'd been skirting danger for two weeks, getting caught, getting loose . . . Our luck was sure to run out, eventually.

Looks like it just did.

The bay reached the trees in a full gallop. Too late, I fought him, tried to pull him up, tried to slow him down. The path wound around a large tree, then dropped down at a steep decline. At the bend, a large tree root jutted up. My horse couldn't see it in the dark and I remembered it was there, too late. Going too fast to miss it, the bay tripped.

We went over. I was thrown, far off the path.

The ground felt incredibly hard. My head cracked . . . and the black night fell away into a swirling, nightmarish nothing . . .

Sometime later, I was vaguely aware of rough hands, turning

me, lifting me up. I tried to kick, to cry out . . . wasn't sure if my foot had moved or if the sounds coming from my mouth were anywhere near as loud as the screaming rage inside my head.

That someone knew my name, called me out loud.

"Kathy. Wake up."

The pounding in my head nauseated me. I couldn't see. My arm . . . too tired . . . wouldn't raise . . . couldn't fight back.

That same rough hand held my face, covering my mouth and jaw . . . And again, that voice, so familiar, called my name. "Kathy?"

I tried to answer, to speak around those strong fingers.

"Hmngnith."

"It's no use. She's out cold."

That voice! I'd know it anywhere. Even without her raucous bark, I would have recognized the quick toss of my body over a shoulder, methodically and efficiently preparing to dispose of a nuisance. Albeit it was of the human species.

Ranger Woman.

"Throw her on the horse," she said. ". . . and let's head back to the cabin. I'm cold."

Again, those rough hands picked me up and draped me like a rag doll over the back of the bay, my hair tangling in the saddle, twisting my head to one side.

It was daylight before I realized I was inside a room. A very familiar room. I'd been gaining consciousness by degrees when I became aware of Casey. He was on the floor, back to the wall, tied, and studying my face with great concern. "Kath?" he said. "You OK?"

I'd been dumped in the corner, also on the floor, a good three yards away from him. I was thirsty and my head felt like a semi had entered it through one ear, unloaded, and drove out the other side.

Again, the voice, a very unfeminine, female voice, said, "Well, well, well. Is Miss High and Mighty awake?"

"What do you want?"

Ranger Woman stood before us, obviously enjoying herself. "I want the truth and I want it now."

I paused, puzzled as to what the term 'truth' actually meant to this woman.

Casey was quietly watching her every move.

"Fess up, you two. What the hell are you doing here? And don't give me any more bull about being campers, out for a weekend away from the office. If that was the case, you'd have been long gone the first time you had a horse under you." She moved closer, her silver-tipped cowboy boots just inches away. Each end of the boot had been overlaid by a silver plate, creating a hard-as-a-hammer heel and a lethal looking point at the toe. "So tell me who you're working for and who else knows you're up here or I swear, I'll kick your brains out."

I tried looking up at her and winced from the effort. I had to tell her something . . . anything that would keep those boots pinned to the floor. "You're right," I said, forcing a cough, my head spinning from the pain and the need to make up a story on the spot. "I'm from the . . . *this would have to be good* . . . Federal Unconditional Compensation for Kids." I thought of how the first letters of each word would spell out and almost laughed out loud in spite of the headache. "You're right. I am an investigator. Hired to find the children and grandchildren of the Fordham downwinders. People, such as yourself who suffered damage, both physically and emotionally, from the toxic emissions of Fordham Nuclear Waste. Casey was hired to my guide and bodyguard."

"Sure. And I'm Joan of Arc. Want to see my shield?"

"There are a lot of imposters and we had to make sure you were not one of them. After talking to you and seeing the effects on your brother Jimmy, I'm convinced you have legal grounds. How about you, Casey?"

He nodded, dumbly, pursed his lips, and dropped his eyes to the floor.

She squinted at me and hoisted a hand to one hip. "What does that mean?"

"It means that, upon my return to the office, I will submit the necessary reports and documents to see that your family is reimbursed for everything you've been through. Monetarily."

"You said you were gonna have to turn me in. What about that?"

"Ah, yes. I won't lie to you."

At least no more than you would to me. And I certainly would never hide behind the Bible to do it. "You will be questioned about it. But, once they hear the whole story from me, what I actually saw there in that house before it burned down, there will

164

be no question as to who has what coming." I smiled, as charmingly as possible, considering the circumstances.

"You're lying. Think you can get me to turn your ass loose and let you go. Just like that. Well, if you think I can be fooled that easy, you got another think coming."

Behind her, the outside door creaked, boots thudded across the kitchen and an armful of wood clattered onto the floor. A two-foot length of fir, cut for firewood, rolled into the doorway.

Loren, the old boy we'd come to know as Whiskers, was back. He wore the same outdated Marlboro jacket, a little the worse for wear, and on his feet were a not-so-new pair of grey lizard-skin cowboy boots. Some terribly familiar cowboy boots. In fact, the same cowboy boots I'd shuffled in, all the way up from our camp to the compound. They'd been fished from the lake, right next to Johnny's dead carcass.

Ranger Woman seemed glad to see him. "Loren, our little friend here says she's from some agency that wants to pay us for our loss."

"What loss?"

"You know. The farm, Mom and Dad dying, Jimmy all messed up, that sort of thing."

He entered the room and stood next to Ranger Woman. A black leather saddle bag hung from one hand. "Balderdash. They're spies. Sent here to investigate our whole set-up." He stomped over in front of me. "All we want to know is, what's your schedule? Who else knows you're up here and how long have you got to finish the job before your boss, or whatever they call him, sends out a posse to retrieve your skinny ass. And please. Don't give me any lip. I'm in no mood for it."

Arguing with this man would not help. I had to think and I had to be right. "Two weeks," I answered. "And that would be stretching it."

"Two weeks. Starting from . . ."

"From the time we left." Straining at the ropes they'd used to tie my hands, by pure habit, I went to look at the date on my watch. Too late, I remembered I'd left it in the Porsche that same night we drove up from Seattle. Although it seemed like years since we'd left the boundaries of civilization, it was probably closer to ten or eleven days. "I don't even know for sure what day it is, but I'm sure they're really beginning to wonder why I haven't checked in yet."

"Today is the fourteenth of September."

I nodded as if I wasn't the least bit surprised. In fact, after all Casey and I had been through, the earth beneath our feet could crumble like last year's cookie and not elicit more, on this day, than a yawn. "I expect a search party at any time."

"And how about your boyfriend here. Is he expected to get back to headquarters? I don't believe you're high enough on the totem pole to be given free rein to investigate without at least some sort of supervision."

I laughed, both at their fumbling efforts to umask their idea of a super sleuth and at my boyfriend's sullen expression. "Casey? Oh, no. He's just a . . . I mean, Casey's no investigator. He's manager of the produce department at Groceries Plus."

Ranger Woman's uniform had been replaced with jeans and a snug cowboy shirt, her red hair tied up under a straw hat. I wondered if she'd already resigned from the Park Service or been fired. She bent down and flicked my chin with her thumb, forcing me to look into her cold, green eyes. It was like staring into the ocean waters, out deep where you couldn't see the bottom. "Don't kid yourself, Lady," she said, swaggering over to Casey's side, hips swaying in the tight jeans. "Johnny told me about his little brother, lots of times. About how they used to play detective when they were kids, some kind of kooky version of cowboys and Indians, and how they both grew up to be FBI informants. Johnny got him the job after he became Chief of some group or another. Oh, yea. He told me all about it. But, instead of turning us in, Casey said he'd help. A turncoat, I guess you'd call it. He was the one showed us how to fake the paperwork, stamp it with these seals and stuff. Even brought us the official forms to use." She leered over him. "Isn't that right, Casey? Up here looking for big brother? Didn't get your share of the take last time?"

As Janice paced the room, thoroughly enjoying the attention, I began to realize what had been bothering me. I had yet to hear the buzz of a single Forest Service plane or helicopter. I'd expected it, listened for it, but they still hadn't shown up. And the fact that Janice was on the force would never have stopped them from investigating the huge fire from the burning house. Somehow, someone had made the airspace above the compound off

166

limits. And no state agency that I was aware of, had that much power. It had to be a federal decree.

Janice was still hauling Casey over the coals. "Jack said he saw you in a red pickup, hanging around the lake. What was it? About a week, week and a half before you came back with this little blond bombshell?"

Casey? Was here ... at the lake ... before? Then brought me up?

I didn't believe her. Refused to believe her. After all, the woman had exhibited some pretty wild behavior. Almost schizophrenic. Switching from one personality to another the way I might change my blouse. One minute, she was Miss Goody Two Shoes, spouting Bible verses and clucking over Jimmy like a mother hen. The next minute, she was a full-blown psychotic, dripping sex-appeal and ready to have us all killed.

As we'd all come to expect, Casey said nothing. The only visible response to Janice's outlandish accusations was the way his lips gathered to the side in deep thought, his dark hair almost covering the quick black eyes.

It was Loren's turn to be rude. "Now, before you tell us you're not going to answer our questions," he said. "You need to understand just how dispensable you are. You and your scrawny friend, have been nothing but a real pain in the butt. So, keep in mind, that we're here to be convinced that we should let you hang around. Instead of an unfortunate accident. Now. Tell us, while you can still talk naturally and before I'm forced to give you something to prod your memory banks. Where'd you hide the disk, Casey?"

He shook his head a definite 'NO', glancing first at me. He wasn't talking.

Loren began fumbling in the saddle bag. I held my breath, knowing I wouldn't like whatever he had in there. "Well," he said, and brought out a large syringe, of the type I'd seen doctors use to give shots. "Let's see if we can help you loosen that tongue of yours a little. Get your memory banks fired up." To Janice, or Ranger Woman, or whoever she was at that moment, he commanded, "Hold him down."

Poor Casey. They converged on him like vultures. I had no idea what was in that needle but it had to be a drug of some type and I couldn't handle waiting to watch Casey's reaction in order to find out what kind. "Wait!" I shouted, louder than I needed.

Loren paused, and stared at me. "I'll tell you. Sure. We found the disk, even tried it in the computer upstairs. I couldn't get past the password. It was left there in the computer room, burned up with everything else."

"You're lying. If you hadn't read anything on there, or seen any of the paper copies, you never would have come back to this cabin. You'd have been long gone down the mountain towards home."

His attitude was infuriating. And although Casey had motioned to me to keep mum and was even following his own advice, I couldn't let this last insult go by without comment. "And you would have had us killed on the way. Easy, quick, and hard to trace. Isn't that right? Isn't that where Jack's been most of the time? Hidden on some stretch of trail, waiting to shoot us in the back as we fled?"

"Mouthy little broad, aren't you? Well, if you know so much why don't you tell me how does Janice know so much about your little lover. Tell her, Janice. About Casey's feeble efforts at putting the moves on you while he hid out in Cashmere as an apple-picker. Think we didn't know what you were up to Sonny Boy?"

Casey? An FBI informant AND Ranger Woman's exlover? "You're lying," I said with a weakening bluster, trying to catch my boyfriend's eye, my lover, my FIANCE. "If Casey knew either one of you before, he would have told me long ago."

As usual, Casey was sullen, noncommunicative, and a real brat. He wouldn't speak, he wouldn't deny it, and he wouldn't even look at me.

"Oh, but that's not all. While Sonny Boy was swearing his eternal love to Janice, he was also trying to get her to reveal the details of our going concern up here. Ha! Thought you had us fooled, didn't you, Casey? We knew all the while who you were, who your brother WAS, and who you were feeding information to. Oh. Did we forget to mention, that the information you got, had very little to do with actual facts?"

"Sorry, Loren," I said, shaking my head with what I hoped would pass for total conviction. "I'm not buying it." But in the quiet recesses of my own mind, I was troubled. Unbidden, memories of the times I had caught Casey looking through some of my papers, asking questions, seemingly with honest curiosity. Although I'd thought at the time, his naivete' was a little much, even for him, I'd been willing to take him at his word. He'd even tried to use my computer to look up a recipe, he'd claimed, and I just happened to catch him reading a file I'd brought home from work. That file was full of Darrian's notes. Some he'd made as the prosecuting attorney on a case pending against Fordham. A case brought by a group of Fordham's downwinders, now living in Spokane. Again, Casey'd pleaded an innocent if dumb mistake, and again, I'd believed him, although I was really beginning to wonder how he'd managed to get that far into a file without my help. Supposedly, he hadn't a clue as to the inner workings of a computer.

The idea that I, a mere woman, might challenge the Great Doctor and literally, call him a liar, seemed to inflame Loren. He'd become fixated on the need to convince me he was all-powerful, all wise, and thereby rule his little world with great power and control. "OK. Try this one. Janice, maybe she'd like to see that picture you have of Johnny. Where is it?," he demanded, as if she was expected to produce his every desire on the spot and was dangerously close to a full blown rage if he didn't get it.

She stared at him, close-mouthed, and I could see the beginnings of fear. Her fear, his fury.

She didn't trust Loren much more than I did.

Agitated, he began to pace back and forth, his voice rising. To me, he said, "The family resemblance really is striking." To Janice, he said, almost shouting, "I need that picture, Janice. Would you bring it here? PLEASE."

"Uh, I . . . guess its still at the house . . . was at the house . . .

"At the house? You mean you let it burn?"

"I didn't LET anything burn, Loren. The house burned down. Period. I didn't ask it to and I couldn't stop it. It just burned. And so did everything inside." She glared at him, green eyes flashing.

"Well. Then there's only one thing left to do. We'll have to get Casey here to tell the truth. And I have just the thing to assist him in recalling a little of his own past." Delving into the saddlebags he'd brought in with him, Loren pulled out a needle and began to fill it from a little bottle. "A little shot of sodium pentathol ought to do the trick. Janice, when I give the word, hold him still. This needs to be inserted directly into a vein."

Fighting two against one and tied to boot, Casey didn't have much of a chance. Ranger Woman pinned him to the floor while

Loren prepared the needle.

They're going to kill him. I had to do something. "If that's true, that Casey really was related to that cowboy, it still doesn't prove a thing. Other than maybe Casey was trying to find his brother. It doesn't mean he was the one who killed him. In fact, I would think it proves just the opposite. That he was hoping to find his murderer."

"You stay out of this. Or maybe you'd like a little happy juice, yourself."

Casey put up a good fight. No one could have asked him to fight harder. But he was only one man and they were ruthless. Eventually, Janice got tired of having to wrestle with him and still hold his arm perfectly still. She tied his arm to the length of chopped fir Loren had brought in for the wood stove then tightened a thin wire around his throat and threatened to cut off his wind if he moved. Finally, with clenched teeth and closed eyes, Casey stopped struggling and allowed them to have their way.

While they were waiting for the stuff to take effect on Casey, they started for me. "OK. Protocol demands, when you finish with one patient, a good doctor goes directly to the next. No unreasonable waiting periods in this office. Don't worry. A double dose of this stuff ought to put you out of your misery for a long time. A REAL long time."

Either Janice was tiring of her role as nurse or she was too confident that I would be a snap to subdue. As she walked directly toward me, I waited until she was bending over me, poised to grab me by the arm. When she was least expecting it, I rolled over on my back, raised up both feet, and kicked her in the crotch as hard as I could.

She screamed, grabbing herself by the privates. "You little bitch! I'll get you for this."

I would have enjoyed my score more if I hadn't been so vulnerable. But I was the one who was tied, there was still two of them, and Casey was off in never-never land. Muttering and drooling.

Loren simply picked up another chunk of wood and dropped it on the floor next to me. "Sorry, Kathy. I hate having to do this to a woman. But believe it or not, this really is the best way. In ten, twenty minutes, you'll go to sleep. That's all. There won't be any pain and you'll never know what happened." He glanced at

Janice. "All right," he said. "Let's get this over with. I haven't eaten all day and my blood sugar's down."

My kick had slowed her down but only momentarily. She came at me, smacking my face with a vengeance and twisting my arm to the back hard enough to break it. I too screamed, helpless against their evil and frightened to the core.

Aloof and indifferent, Loren waited, needle refilled and poised to plunge its poison into my arm. It wasn't long before my struggling had used up every ounce of energy I had. I felt the prick of the needle, the final twist of my arm that convinced me to hold still or suffer a dislocated shoulder. "Oh, don't. Please don't."

"Damn it," Loren said, jabbing me numerous times, wrenching my arm each time I kicked or cried out. "I always hated this part of doctoring. That's why I went into science." Suddenly, he withdrew the needle. "Hold her down," he demanded, and got up. "Do you have any elastic? Any of those big rubber bands? I'll need something to bind her upper arm. I can't find her main artery and the others keep collapsing." If I had any luck this day, it would be that Loren was having trouble capturing a vein. He wouldn't be able to inject the drug without it.

Meanwhile, Casey was babbling and though most of it was incoherent, I was sure I heard the name, 'Johnny,' at least once. He seemed to be repeating a conversation between them that had been held sometime in their past. They were arguing over a gun. It was terribly sad, and sounded as if Casey were truly mourning for his brother. I wasn't sure, but I thought I saw Janice stiffen and glance at me guiltily.

From what I'd seen so far, that poor dead cowboy was the key to more than one mystery. Just the mention of his name seemed to unlock Janice's ability to act, somewhat, like the daughter her parents had raised. Her whole demeanor seemed to change on the spot.

She must have loved Johnny, very much.

Loren walked over to the pantry and began rifling through the shelves and drawers. Janice followed him. I could hear them whispering, she seemed to be asking him questions, he seemed to be angry at having to answer them.

" . . . How about some wire?" he growled. "Do you have any wire in this damn hovel?"

More whispering.

171

Could Ranger Woman actually be trying to save my life? I wasn't sure, but she'd suddenly changed her whole attitude and it seemed as if she was now trying to talk Loren out of killing me. Maybe she was afraid of getting caught. Kidnapping was one thing, murder one was another. Or, maybe she felt obliged to carry out her vow to me, for saving little Jimmy. They negotiated more. Quietly, and out of earshot.

A few minutes later, inflamed from his own suppressed passions, Loren's voice went on the rise. I still couldn't hear Janice, but his was louder and I was able to catch phrases of his side of the squabble. "But . . .," he said, agitated to the max. "These two are investigators. Cheap, back room, peeping toms. Spies, Janice."

Evidently, Janice had decided it was time for the ultimate weapon. From the corner of my eye I could see her press her body up next to his, playing with the buttons on his shirt.

He began a plea for mercy. " . . . Janice . . . Honey . . .,"

Loren didn't have a chance. He fought bravely and with his all, thrusting his ego into the foray like the spears of old warriors and confronted Janice's uprising head-on. "I cannot permit this . . .," he choked, arms encircling her low enough to fondle her rump, each hand kneading a meaty cheek. " . . . this coddling of our . . . our prisoners . . ." Loren obviously thought he could reason with her, but he was no match for her kind of warfare. "We've got to know what she knows," he whimpered, with much heavy breathing. In my mind's eye, I could see his backbone turn to mush. With her hand inside his shirt, stroking his hairless chest, he set aside the needle and pulled her up and into him. As she giggled, giving him a quick bump, I felt embarrassed for us all and turned my eyes away, marveling that they could do all of this without ever getting undressed.

I heard them kiss, wetly and passionately. Finally, he broke away to breathe deeply, and said, as if it were an afterthought, "I really should give her at least a partial dose." But, by now, he was on the offensive and loosing ground. Mumble, mumble, more kissing. Then, "All right," he blurted. "Have it your way. But don't ever say I didn't tell you what was best, if and when the little bitch gets away and rats on us all."

Chapter

19

"Now," Loren said, grumpy at Janice's sudden withdrawal from their lovemaking in the name of having to tend to business. To her, he said, "Shall we interrogate our little friend, Casey while he's under the influence? Or do you have objections to that, too?"

She shrugged and shook her head. "No. I have no objections to that. Should I?" Once again, she'd gotten her way and was becoming bored with the whole scheme. Thank goodness, her way was contributory to the notion that I might remain alive.

Having gained Ranger Woman's permission, Loren stepped to Casey's side and kicked him. "Hey. Casey. Wake up."

"Hugnth."

"I said to wake up, damn it." Again, Loren drew back his foot, taking aim, the sharp toe of the cowboy boot poised for serious damage.

But Janice had stepped between the boot and Casey. "I'll do it. Let me talk to him."

"Damn it, Janice. Do you have to interfere with everything I try to do? I'm trying to interrogate this man, if you'll get out of the way."

"Yes, I do have to interfere, Loren. When it means that you're trying to bash the guy's ribs in for no reason. What would we do with him then, huh? How would you like to try getting him off this mountain if he can't even ride a horse? Eventually, you're going to have to either let them go or kill them. And I've told you before, Loren. I'm not a killer. Taking another human life goes against the Ten Commandments more than any of the others. Don't you see? I'm thinking about us. And the thought of having three murder raps hanging over your head is more than I can take. And mine too, by the way. Since I'm here, I'm also involved. But I guess you don't mind having ME rot in prison."

Loren looked shocked. "Hey, Doll. Who said you were going to prison? Come here," he said and folded her into his arms. "Now, you know that's not true. Did you really think I'd let any of those assholes touch one hair on your pretty head? As soon as we're finished here, we're heading for . . ." Glancing at me, Loren dropped his voice a few decibels. He finished his discussions with Janice with his head buried in her hair, his lips caressing her ear as he whispered. She seemed to be whispering in a negotiating sort of way more than recovering from hurt feelings, but I doubted Loren could see that. In fact, I doubted Loren could see much of anything, as each time he tried to regain a part of his manhood, it was cut down with a slash of green eyes and burned alive by a headfull of flaming red hair. When that didn't work, a pair of bouncy boobs stood ever-ready to smother him in ecstasy.

After a few minutes of touchy-feely negotiations, Janice seemed satisfied with what she'd achieved and resumed her normal tone of voice. " . . . especially, since Casey has pals who know where he went and may have a search party out looking for him as we speak. That's what I'm worried about. That sort of thing."

"All right. Get it over with, then. He's not going to stay under forever, you know."

Janice then sauntered, hips swinging a wide path, over to Casey and knelt down. He was sprawled out on the floor, drifting in and out of sleep, a look of placid indifference on his face. "Casey, honey," she said, softly shaking his shoulder.

"Hmnignth."

She'd purposely placed her back to me so I couldn't see the sentiment that passed between them. "It's Janice, Honey. Remember me?"

Hearing it was bad enough.

Brother or no brother, Casey had been lying to me all along.

"I need to ask you some questions. OK?"

"Hmnignth. Whnkindakessons?"

"Some questions about Johnny. Think about Johnny for a minute, OK? Your half brother?"

"Johnny. I . . . Johnny. Shot. Hurry! By the lake!"

"That's right, Johnny was by the lake. Now, Casey, you need to tell me. Did you know Johnny was up here on the compound with me? Did you know that BEFORE you came up here to camp out?"

"Johnny. Johnny needed help. Someone after him. Guns. Computer disks. Said for me to come, to ride out with him to Tri-cities."

"That's right, Casey. You're doing real good. Just a few more questions, OK? OK, Casey? Can you stay awake for me? Please?"

"Hmnignth."

"Now, I need to find out about the disk, Casey. Did you find it? Did Johnny have the disk in his saddle bags?"

"Disk. Computer disk. Hmnignth. Rice. Too much rice."

"Yes, Casey. Pay attention, now. I need to know about the disk. Where is the computer disk. Did you find it?"

Evidently, Casey nodded. Janice had grown extremely excited, causing Loren to try to get in the act. "Casey," he demanded. "Tell Janice about the disk. Where's the damn disk, Casey?"

"Get back, Loren. You're confusing him."

But Casey had already espied his assailant and whatever Janice and he had going, it was over. Including any further revelations he might have made. They were now overridden by fear of Loren. "No!" He cried, staring wild-eyed. "Go away." Scrambling to get away from Loren, Casey pulled and tugged at the ropes that held him. "I have to go now. I'm going." Knowing it was going all wrong, Loren grabbed Casey, trying to reason with him, to calm him down. It didn't work. Casey seemed to be operating on one track at a time. And that track was now focused on Loren and the pain he had caused. "You hurt. Needles. Go away."

Janice got up. "It's no use," she sighed, and shoved Loren back into the kitchen. "Let him sleep it off and we'll try again later."

Knowing he'd shown his butt not only to Janice but also in front of me, Loren reacted in the same way he'd been reacting for some time. He turned, spotting me on the floor. Thin lips twisting behind the slit of grey beard, he made a motion as if he'd like to kick me also into tomorrow and growled, "What are you looking at?"

I shrank against the wall, preferring to pick my fights a little more carefully, and pretended to be subdued. I was afraid he'd carry out his threats and even braced myself for the cut of that pointed, but Janice beckoned to him from the other room. He left, shaking a finger as if to say, 'Just you wait. I'll be back . . . later.'

This time, they huddled in the kitchen. Whispering . . . smooching . . .

Watching them in the act of their awful deeds was scary enough. But with them out of sight and hearing range and knowing they would return having hatched some kind of diabolical scheme, was even worse. A cold chill scampered up my back and across my shoulder. There was no way to guess as to what their next move might be. I strained on the ropes that tied my wrists together until I felt blood ooze down my hand.

But I couldn't hear a single word.

Finally, frightfully, the sounds changed. There seemed to be a determination, a verdict as to our sentence. I could hear Loren clump across the kitchen and Janice snap at him. Both voices raised in anger, and I heard him say, "No, damn it. We've gone this far, and I'm not going to let them screw it up now. Maybe things are getting too rough for you. If so, you better go on. Go and get your brothers ready to travel. I'll take care of things here and be about an hour behind you." The outside door creaked open and I could hear their mumbling goodbyes.

Then . . . I waited . . .

Within minutes, the sound of horses stomping and blowing came in through the open door . . .

Janice's leaving. OH, God. We'll be left here alone with Loren!

But it wasn't her departure I heard. It was an arrival.

Jack burst into the tiny cabin, pulling the crying Jimmy behind him. "What the shit is this?" Jack demanded. "What you got Kathy on the floor for? I thought we had that all settled. God damn you Loren. I turn my back for one minute and this is what you come up with. Crazy son-of-a-bitch!"

Janice interjected, shaking her head at the suggestion that I might be untied. "Jack," she said. "Settle down and tell me why you dragged Jimmy up here on horseback. You know he hates to ride horses. Look at him. Jimmy, come here and give Sister a hug. Jack, look at him. He's hysterical."

"Tell me about it. I come back from down the road and find Jimmy all alone, scrambling around the damn tack room, scared to death. What was I supposed to do? Just walk out and leave him there like everyone else did? Including you?"

"What do you mean? I left him with Ralph and the others."

"Hey. Ralph and them are history. Long gone. Think they couldn't see the writing on the wall? Hah. Think again." He tramped into the living room and spied me on the floor. "And I want to know what the shit Loren's trying to pull with Kathy."

Jimmy ran in, throwing himself down on top of me, hugging me desperately around the neck and weeping. "Jesus loves me, Jesus loves me."

Loren exploded. "Janice. Get them the hell out of here. How am I supposed to finish things up with a homicidal maniac and a moron on the loose?"

He had angered Jack. "Moron? Maniac? I'll show you, you son-of-a . . ."

"No, Jack. That's not the way to do it. I want you to . . ."

Jack went back outside, then came stomping back in. "I'm gonna kill that . . . that scientific bastard." Evidently, he'd pulled his rifle from the scabbard on his horse. When he came back in, he had a bead on his former whiskered friend.

"No, Jack," Janice said, obviously forcing her voice to sound calm and rational. "Don't shoot. Listen a minute. Listen to me."

While Jack, Loren, and Janice argued, I resumed my efforts at trying to get away. I wasn't sure who she was helping, or even if she knew who she wanted to help, but I didn't feel I wanted to wait and find out.

Jimmy had thrown himself on the floor, his head burrowed in my arm pit. "Jimmy," I said. "Can you help? I need your help, Jimmy." He raised his head, quizzically. "Can you untie me? There. The ropes on my wrists. Try to untie them, OK?"

For a few minutes, poor Jimmy plucked at the ropes, baffled as to the inner workings of a square knot. But the violence and name-calling from outside was more than he could handle. Crestfallen, he threw himself down on the floor next to me and whimpered, "I can't. Jimmy stupid. Stupid, stupid, stupid." He began to sob.

"No, you're not stupid, Jimmy. Don't you believe him. OK? It's not true. Jimmy's a little slow and it's hard for him to pay attention. But he's not stupid. Jimmy's smart. OK? Promise me you won't ever believe anyone who says any different. Promise?"

He nodded, his soft pink lips quivering and turned down at the corners.

"Tell me you promise not to believe them. OK?" I hated to speak to the guy in the second person, but he'd obviously been talked about, in his presence, more than he'd been spoken to. "Jimmy has to promise he won't believe Loren when he says mean things, OK?"

"OK. Jimmy promise."

"And what is Jimmy?" To help him out, I mouthed the words several times. "Say it for Kathy. Jimmy is . . ."

"Jimmy smart," he said, beaming with pride.

"See there? You know, don't you?" Again, he nodded with a surprising amount of comprehension and pouted, showing me how much he'd been hurt. At last, I was getting somewhere. "Don't forget. Loren is bad and stupid. Not Jimmy. Jimmy smart. OK. Jimmy, I have to ask you something. And you'll have to talk to me. Can you do that? Can you answer some questions?"

With a bright-eyed interest, Jimmy assured me he could.

"Jimmy, remember when I was using the computer? And you were so smart, when you told me all those numbers?"

Again, he responded with full concentration. "Yes. Jimmy remembers."

"Good, Jimmy. You're doing great. Now, this is important. Did you hear Loren say those numbers out loud? All of them?"

He gestured nervously to the quarreling three-some, big-eyed and blinking. "Jimmy was watching Loren work on computer. He was saying numbers. I asked him if I could play. I could maybe learn. But Loren get mad. Say Jimmy too stupid to work."

"But Loren was wrong, wasn't he? Loren's stupid, because he doesn't know."

Poor Jimmy. He was now gazing at me like a lost puppy-dog.

All right. Now, I'll tell you what. I want you to look in my shirt pocket." With my chin, I tried to indicate my top left. "Look

178

in there. It's a surprise. Jimmy like surprises? Jimmy, you. You like surprises?" Blue eyes bright and full of hope, I had his full attention. "There's a surprise in my pocket. Can you get it out?"

"Surprise," he said, his round cheeks beaming with glee. "Birthday. Jimmy has a birthday."

"That's right. Look in my pocket for Jimmy's birthday."

Meanwhile, the fight raged on. By now, Janice seemed to have sided with Jack against Loren. "No, Jack. Don't shoot. Tie him up, yes. But don't shoot him yet." I didn't trust her, and evidently, neither did her own brother.

"Why not," Jack demanded. "Give me one good reason why I shouldn't kill the son-of-a-bitch!"

At least they weren't paying us any attention. Jimmy had the can of cayenne pepper out and was prying the top off. "That's right, Jimmy. But be careful. Don't let it be too close to your face, OK? Hold it way out away from your face. That's the way. Good boy, Jimmy. You're doing great."

Meanwhile, Loren had pounced on Jack and was wrestling him for the rifle. More cursing, more epithets of what each would do should they get what they wanted which was to choose their weapons and their means of torture of the other.

Jimmy had momentarily stopped playing with the can and was mesmerized, watching them fight. "Hey, Jimmy," I said, drawing him back to the task at hand. "Pay attention. OK? OK, Jimmy?"

Bright eyes trained back on me, he again began to babble. "Jesus loves me. Jimmy's birthday. Surprise."

"That's right, Jimmy. And we're going to have a surprise. Now, I want you to take that can, be careful with it now. DO NOT SMELL THE CAN, JIMMY. Keep it away from your face. There you go. Now, pay attention Jimmy. OK? Listen very, very carefully. This is what I want you to do. This is the surprise, OK?"

"Jimmy has a birthday. Surprise present."

"That's right. We're going to have a surprise. But I need your help, Jimmy. Jimmy? OK? Can Jimmy help Kathy have a surprise?"

"Jimmy smart. Jesus loves me, this I know."

"Yes, Jimmy's very smart. And Jesus loves me too, OK? Are you paying attention?"

He nodded, not bothering to answer, giving me his full attention. I felt like I'd won a small victory. Loren seemed to be overpowering Jack with a few well placed karate kicks and Janice seemed unable to do much more than scream at the both of them. Even so, Jimmy pointedly ignored them, taking in my every word and gesture.

"Jimmy, I want you to do something. Something very important. I need your help, Jimmy. Loren has tied me up, and I can't get loose."

Immediately, he dove behind me, again plucking at the rope on my wrists. Hopefully, he hadn't upset the cayenne pepper in the process. "No, Jimmy. Come up here in front where I can see you. Oh, God. Where's the can, Jimmy. The surprise. Let me see the surprise can. NO, don't put it in my face, just let me see it. OK. Careful don't spill it. Listen carefully, now. Here's what you do. Jimmy. Jimmy must do. Go over to Loren, see there where he's holding Bubba with the rope? Soon, Bubba will be tied up just like I am. Bubba get tied up like Kathy."

Jimmy was hyperventilating. "Jimmy, stop it. Don't breathe that way. Do it right." Poor Jimmy. He had known violence, probably more than his share and I was sure he had never before participated in it. But without his help, we were all doomed. "Listen, now. Kathy needs help. Jimmy help Kathy. Listen to Kathy. Jimmy can help. Jimmy throw the surprise can in Loren's face. Loren hurt Kathy and he hurt Bubba. Hurry, Jimmy. Help Kathy. Jimmy go now. Go over to Loren and throw the surprise can in his face. Go, Jimmy. Go for God's sake!"

He blinked and looked at the can.

He may not be capable of it. Of understanding the act he would take or, even if he did, of causing pain in another human being.

Loren had knocked Jack senseless and was now elbowing Ranger Woman out of the way so he could tie him. It was now or never. "Go, Jimmy. Throw the can at Loren. Hurry."

It was a miracle. Jimmy proceeded to get up, a grim determination seeming to harden his soft features, and marched over to Loren. He had to be looking straight at him when Loren bashed Janice in the jaws with his elbow, sending her flying backwards.

Jimmy screamed and I, from my seat on the floor, screamed with him. "Loren bad, Jimmy smart. Loren bad, Jimmy smart."

And as if he were sent to be the Gillespie family's avenging angel, he stationed himself directly in front of Loren, threw up his chubby little arm, and covered those whiskers with cayenne pepper.

Chapter

20

The effect of the pepper didn't last long, but it was long enough. It gave Ranger Woman and Jack the moment they needed to recover and tie Loren with his own rope. It wasn't long before Janice produced the needle of sodium pentathol and revealed why she'd kept him from shooting it into me. She wanted to save it for Loren. "It's damn time we found out, once and for all, what he really did to our father."

21

I couldn't believe it. We were actually going home.

Headed down off the mountain. Finally.

Loren was tied on a horse, having had admitted his all at Fordham. His experiments that had unquestionably caused the malignant tumors that killed their parents and many others.

He'd also admitted his killing of Johnny. For a man with his connections, it hadn't been hard at all for him to get an account on Johnny's actual occupation. Casey had him in tow, keeping a wary eye and a loaded carbine, determined to get him to the proper authorities.

Of course, any prosecutor would have only our say-so as to what happened up there in that line cabin, but he had only to look at Loren's history and I still had the disk tucked neatly away in my camera case. And the snapshots, and the paper reports I'd saved from the fire. With all of that, Darrian should have a pretty tight case.

Evidently, Johnny had indeed been smuggling the disk out, having been hired by the new Secretary of Energy to investigate the missing nuclear waste. Which explained the 'hands-off' handling by the Forest Service. Janice had supposedly been hired to patrol the grounds alone, and radio out if she needed help.

Casey had been going to ride out with his brother, as a kind of back-up. They'd planned to meet at the rocks, about a week before our ill-fated camping trip. When he never showed, Casey had been at a loss as to how to carry on. As he also knew about Darrian's case and actually wanted to help him win, Casey decided I would need to see the lake, notice the dead stuff, and take a sample of the water back to be tested. It was the only way he knew how to get a Federal investigation going without wasting precious time. Which would have run into months.

He'd actually known about Darrian's law suit before I did. The agency Johnny had worked for were the plaintiffs.

We passed the dead lake and the Porsche. At least my car hadn't moved or been pilfered from since I'd left it . . .

How long ago? Two weeks? A little more?

Seemed more like a year.

After a hasty once-over and a quick kick of the tires, we went back to the trail and on to the Ranger Station. Jack and Janice/Ranger Woman seemed docile enough, riding along behind for several miles without being forced, leading Jimmy's horse.

At a fork in the trail, they stopped.

"Sorry," Janice said, reining her horse in. "But this is where we part company."

I wasn't surprised. Hadn't really expected them to change their spots into prisoners stripes, overnight. "Where will you be going?" I asked her, more out of pure habit than curiosity.

"Canada's just a few hours from here. Don't know what we'll do once we get there. I've got enough saved up, that we can get by for awhile."

"Well," I said to her and to Jack. "I don't know what to say. Do I thank you for saving our lives when Loren would have taken them? Or do I curse you for getting us in that mess in the first place? We never would have made it out of there without your help."

"You know," Janice replied, propping an elbow on the saddle horn. "If you think about it, we weren't the ones who got you in that mess. You did. You and Casey. With your snooping and prying into something that wasn't any of your business. But once you were there, we had to deal with you the best we could." She paused, giving me one of her green-eyed stares. "Don't try to stop us, Kathy. It won't work."

"I don't have any intentions of stopping you. In a way, I don't blame you for how you feel and what you've had to do. Under the same circumstances, I'd be tempted to do the same thing. Go on your way. Be happy, for crying out loud."

Jack had already commandeered the mule, packed with supplies, a few miles back. He blushed and stammered, overcome with a sudden shyness. I waited, giving him time, pretending to brush some dust off the bay gelding's neck. After a few false starts, he managed to express himself. "Well," he said, wiping his nose on a gloved hand, peering out at me from under that ridiculous hat he wore. "Janice ain't gonna say nothin' so I guess I'm gonna have to. Kathy, you helped us much more than we ever did you. You reminded us of Mamma. How she raised us, the things she always tried to teach us before she died. And I'll always be grateful to you for that." He nodded, the brim of his hat flopping like big, brown wings, and said, "You take it easy now, you hear? I'll be seeing you around." And before I could reply, off they went, heading north, their horses soon disappearing in a thick growth of trees and bushes.

The last I heard of the Gillespie family, was Jimmy's singing. It was louder than usual, and I wondered how the sound of it could carry all over the mountain top and from so far away until I realized all three Gillespies had joined him. Joyously and in full voice.

"Jesus loves me, this I know . . ."

That night, Casey and I made camp one last time. We'd be reaching the Ranger Headquarters sometime the next afternoon.

It was time to make some decisions about our future.

Together, or apart — what was it going to be?

"Kathy," he said, "You got to believe me, I never knew Johnny was dead when I took you up there. Finding him in them rocks was just about the last thing I ever would have imagined. I knew he was in trouble from Loren and all, but I had no idea I'd be placing you in danger. I just wanted you to see the condition of that lake, maybe take some samples, and report it back to Darrian. I swear, Kath, that's all I ever intended to do. I been trying to get a federal investigation going for months. Now, maybe Darrian'll listen to you. I never thought I'd be putting you in a position to get hurt. Course, I should'a known . . . but I didn't. So, there it is. Will you ever forgive me for being such a dumb-ass?"

"Casey, Honey, there's no need to apologize. I know you didn't mean for all this to happen. How could anybody know?" I patted his hand, gave him a quick peck on his thin cheek. "You did the best you could, under the circumstances. As we all did. Don't worry about it."

"But," he said, swallowing, playing with the fingers on my hand, hinting he wanted me closer . . . "Things have changed between us. I guess it can't be helped, but," he gazed at me, his black button eyes pleading . . . "The thing is, I feel like I'm losing you. And, it just . . . hurts."

"Casey, you and I, we're so different . . ." For some reason, I couldn't stand having to look at him. "You know, there seems to be an opening for a new Forest Ranger in this area. If I were you, I'd put in for it."

"How about you, Kath? I got to know. Are you with me? Will you live here and be my wife?"

Drawing my hand away, gently but firmly, I hugged myself around the knees, took a deep breath, and said, "I . . . don't think so, Casey. I'll always love you in a way, but, frankly, we just don't have enough in common. And I could never stand to live in the boonies for any length of time."

As I expected, his head dropped, and he was once again lost in contemplation. Somewhere in his own little world. Private and unapproachable.

I playfully poked him in the side. "Say, did I tell you? I've put in for a new job opening myself. You know, journalism was my major for the first two years at Kitsap Lutheran College. And I think I've got the job. It's with the Seattle Gazette as a beginning journalist."

THE END